More & More & More Tales to Give You Goosebumps®

Look for the other GOOSEBUMPS
short story collections:

Tales to Give You Goosebumps — Special Edition #1
More Tales to Give You Goosebumps — Special Edition #2
Even More Tales to Give You Goosebumps — Special Edition #3
Still More Tales to Give You Goosebumps — Special Edition #4
More & More Tales to Give You Goosebumps —
Special Edition #5

More & More & More Tales to Give You Goosebumps®

TEN SPOOKY STORIES

R.L.STINE

SCHOLASTIC INC.
New York Toronto London Auckland Sydney

A PARACHUTE PRESS BOOK

ISBN 0-590-36683-1

10 9 8 7 6 5 4 3 2 1

Printed in the U.S.A. 40

First Scholastic printing, October 1997

CONTENTS

More & More & More Tales to Give You Goosebumps®

DON'T SIT ON THE GRONK

"This doesn't work."

"Let me see it, Brad." My fifteen-year-old sister, Kelly, grabbed the Walkman I held in my hands — and nearly yanked my head off.

"Whoa! Wait a second! Let me take the earphones off first!" I yelled.

It was Christmas morning. Mom, Dad, Kelly, and I sat in the living room, around our tree, opening presents.

Mom and Dad bought me the Walkman — but it was definitely broken. No sound came out of the earphones.

"You plugged the earphones into the wrong jack." Kelly frowned at me. "You should have checked the diagram on the box first. You're a total moron."

"I am not a moron!" I yelled.

"Yes, you are!"

"No, I'm not!" I yelled even louder.

"Don't call your brother a moron. It's not nice," Mom scolded Kelly.

"I can't help it if the truth hurts," Kelly declared.

"That's enough," Dad warned her.

I laughed.

Dad turned to me. "Don't laugh. Your sister is right."

Huh?

"You should have looked at the diagram first," he said.

"Your father is right. You never take time to read instructions," Mom said.

"Okay. Okay," I mumbled. "Everyone is right."

I caught Kelly smirking at me as Dad picked up the last present under the tree. "This one is for you, Brad!"

I reached out for the small box wrapped in shiny red paper. I had already opened all my presents. Mom and Dad's should have been the last one.

I checked the card on the box. It said: TO BRAD. But it wasn't signed by anyone.

"Who's this from?" I asked.

No one knew.

I ripped off the paper, opened the box, and peeked inside. "Oh. It's just a Kooshball."

"I'll take it." Kelly grabbed the box from me.

"Give that to me. It's mine!" I grabbed the box back from her.

I have about a hundred Kooshballs — but

there was no way I was letting my stupid sister have anything of mine.

I took the blue Kooshball out of the box.

I wound up — ready to throw it at Kelly.

But I stopped.

Something felt different about this Kooshball.

It felt — warm.

I stared down at it — and gasped.

"Look!" I cried. "It's — it's moving!"

"We're not falling for one of your lame jokes, Brad," Kelly declared.

"I'm telling you — it's moving!"

I studied the ball. It was about the size and weight of a tennis ball. I stared at its blue rubbery strands. Oh — it's not moving, I realized. It's just the strands quivering in my hand. That's what Kooshballs do.

I ran my hand over the strands. They parted — and I saw round bumps underneath. "Hey! Look! This one is different. This must be a new model!"

"You're boring me." Kelly got up and started to leave the room.

I stared at the bumpy ball.

Wait a minute. Did I just see it move?

I squinted at it.

Yes! I did!

"It *is* moving!" I shouted. "It looks like it's breathing!"

Kelly came back into the room. She peered

over my shoulder as I watched the ball. Watched it move in and out. Rising and falling. Small movements — but definitely breathing!

"It's alive!" I cried.

"Drop it!" Kelly cried, backing away. "It *is* alive!"

"Drop it? Are you nuts?" I gently sifted the rubbery strands through my fingers — and the little ball let out a soft purring sound.

"This is too weird!" Kelly backed away some more.

Mom and Dad came over and stared at the ball in the palm of my hand. "It definitely is moving," Mom said.

"It's some kind of creature," Dad said. "I wonder what it is." He scratched his head.

"It's awesome! Can I keep it?" I asked them.

Mom glanced at Dad.

Dad shrugged his shoulders.

"I don't see why not," Mom finally decided. "As long as you take good care of it."

"Cool!" I balanced the creature on top of all my other presents and ran up to my room.

"What *are* you?" I sat on my bed and cradled the creature in my hand. I ran my fingers over its soft, blue spikes — and it let out a giggle!

Whoa!

This was amazing!

I parted the strands and searched for the creature's eyes, its nose, its mouth, its ears.

It didn't seem to have any — at least any that I could see.

I have to call Roscoe and tell him about this, I thought. Roscoe is my best friend. He has a pet hamster that he thinks is incredible. Ha! Wait till he sees this!

I started to place the strange creature back in its box — when I noticed an orange piece of paper on the bottom. I read it out loud: "'How to Take Care of Your Gronk.'"

"So — that's what you are!" I said to the little creature. "You're a Gronk."

I tossed the paper aside. I carefully placed the Gronk back in the box and went to the phone.

When Roscoe heard about the Gronk, he came right over to see it. "Wow! It *is* cool!" he said, staring at the creature in the box.

"Let's take it outside!" I picked up the Gronk, and we ran out to play.

"Let me have it!" Roscoe shouted.

I tossed the creature across my front yard to Roscoe.

"Hey! I think it likes this!" Roscoe caught the creature. "I think I just heard it laugh!"

It was pretty cold out, and I wondered if it was too chilly for the Gronk. But it didn't seem to mind the winter weather at all. Each time we tossed it, it let out a happy little giggle. Totally awesome!

Roscoe threw the Gronk to me — high in the air, way over my head.

Oh, no!

I faded back, back, back — and caught it!

I let out a sigh of relief.

The Gronk wriggled with delight. Its rubber spikes tickled the palms of my hands. "Hey! You're right!" I told Roscoe. "It really does like this!"

We tossed the Gronk back and forth. Back and forth — until I dropped it!

"Nooo!" I gasped as it tumbled out of my hand.

I dove quickly — and caught it before it hit the ground! But something was wrong.

"What happened?" Roscoe jogged up to me.

"It — it got heavy," I stammered. "I dropped it — because I didn't expect it to feel so heavy."

"What do you mean?" Roscoe asked.

"All of a sudden — it feels like it weighs more."

I lifted the Gronk up and down in the palm of my hand. "Yes. It's definitely heavier. Here." I passed the creature to Roscoe. "What do you think?"

Roscoe took the Gronk from me — and let out a cry. "It's growing!"

"No way!" I grabbed the creature back from him — and felt the Gronk's body pulsing in the palm of my hand. Pulsing in and out, with a steady rhythm. Pulsing and growing.

"It is growing!" I gasped.

I watched in awe as the creature's rubbery tendrils wiggled in waves. Wiggled and grew. Longer and longer.

I stood totally still, watching the creature expand in my hands — until it reached the size and weight of a bowling ball.

"Wow! It's really heavy now. Feel it!" I handed the Gronk over to Roscoe. But Roscoe backed off.

The Gronk fell to the ground — and bounced!

"Hey, cool!" I cried.

I caught the Gronk as it bounced up — and dribbled it.

The Gronk let out a loud chuckle!

I passed it to Roscoe.

Roscoe dribbled it, then passed it back to me. The Gronk laughed some more!

I bounced the Gronk up and down my driveway.

The more I dribbled it, the higher it bounced!

The more I dribbled it, the louder it laughed!

"This is amazing!" I shouted as I headed toward the basket that hangs over our garage.

I stepped up to the basket. I took a shot — and scored!

As the Gronk swished through the hoop — it started to grow some more!

"Whoa! It's as big as a basketball now!" I cried.

We shot some hoops with the Gronk.

We played a game of one-on-one. At the end of the game, I caught the creature — and shook my head in disbelief.

"Roscoe, look! It's bigger! It's bigger than a basketball!"

Roscoe didn't know what to say.

We took turns dribbling the Gronk down the block to Roscoe's house — and it continued to grow!

"I have to stop playing." Roscoe wheezed, out of breath. "That thing is too big. And I think it weighs as much as I do."

I stared at the Gronk. It was as big as my huge beach ball. But it was way, way heavier. I bent down and tried to lift it. I couldn't.

"It's kind of creepy." Roscoe gazed down at the Gronk. "I think I'd better go in. It's getting late." He turned and hurried into his house.

I stood behind the Gronk. I leaned over and tried to push it toward my house.

It didn't budge.

I placed both hands firmly against it — and shoved. It slowly started to roll.

Mom and Dad are *not* going to believe the size of this thing, I thought as I pushed the creature.

I couldn't believe it, either. Roscoe was right — it was kind of creepy.

It took all my strength to roll the Gronk back home.

Panting, I pushed harder. "I have to show you to Mom and Dad right away," I said, gazing down at the creature. "I have to show them how fast you're growing. Maybe they can figure out what's going on with you."

By the time I rolled the Gronk to the front door, I was totally out of breath.

I opened the door. Then I leaned against the creature and shoved him inside. "Mom! Dad! Take a look at this!" I shouted. No one came into the room.

"Mom? Dad?" I ran through the house, searching for them. They were gone.

I raced back into the living room.

Oh, no! The Gronk had grown even larger!

I ran into Kelly's room.

"Kelly! Quick! You have to come with me!"

"Can't you see I'm on the phone?" she grumbled.

"*Please!*" I begged.

"Get lost."

I ran back into the living room.

What am I going to do with you? I stared at the creature. You're huge! With a loud grunt, I slowly rolled the Gronk into my bedroom. Then I collapsed on my bed.

The Gronk let out a low purr — and started growing again!

"Wow!" I shouted. "Now you're as big as a chair!"

I jumped out of bed — and sat on it.

"Hey! You're pretty comfortable!" I patted the Gronk. "Like a beanbag chair!"

The Gronk quivered — and giggled.

I pushed myself back and sat deeper into the Gronk.

The Gronk giggled again.

I placed my hands behind my head. I leaned back — and the Gronk rumbled, and grew even more!

Kelly walked by my room without even looking in.

The Gronk continued to swell. It lifted me higher and higher. And higher!

"Stop!" I yelled. "It's too much! Stop growing!"

The Gronk kept growing. Expanding — taking up most of my bedroom floor.

"Please, stop!" I shouted. "You're too big!"

The Gronk continued to grow.

"Kelly — help!"

"What do you want?" Kelly's feet padded down the hall. She turned into my doorway — and shrieked.

"Brad! *What is that?*"

"It's the little creature!" I rolled off the Gronk and fell to the floor. "Only — it's not little anymore!"

I tried to stand. But the creature slapped me hard with its rubbery tendrils — and knocked me down.

Kelly reached out to me — and pulled me toward the door. I squeezed against the Gronk's big body — and finally crawled out into the hall.

"What are we going to do?" I wailed. "It won't stop growing!"

Kelly glanced around my room. Her eyes stopped on the orange sheet of paper on my bed.

She leaned against the Gronk — stretching for the paper. Stretching — until she could grasp it.

"Did you read this?" she demanded, holding up the orange sheet — the instructions that came with the Gronk.

"No. I didn't," I admitted.

The Gronk let out a low chuckle — and swelled some more.

"Let's get out of here!" Kelly grabbed my arm and we ran down the hall.

THUD. THUD. THUD.

The Gronk bounced after us.

"Read the instructions!" I cried as we charged into the living room.

Kelly's voice shook as she read and ran. "'The Gronk will make a delightful pet as long as you follow three simple rules.'"

THUD. THUD. THUD.

The Gronk rolled slowly toward the living room.

"Hurry, Kelly! Read!" I shouted, backing into a corner of the room.

"'Rule number one,'" she read fast. "'The Gronk will keep its tiny size as long as you keep it indoors. NEVER take it outside or it will start to grow rapidly.'"

"Oh, noooo," I moaned.

THUD. THUD. THUD.

The Gronk's bounces grew louder.

"Read!" I cried. "Finish the rules!"

Kelly glanced nervously at the living room doorway. The orange paper trembled in her shaking hands.

"'Rule number two. NEVER use it as a ball because that will make it even more playful than it already is.'"

"Too late!" I cried. "It's too late for that! Keep reading!"

"'Rule number three. NEVER sit on the Gronk because' — *look out, Brad!*" Kelly shrieked and jumped up on the couch.

The Gronk burst into the room. It bounced fast now.

It rolled up to me. It cornered me. It started to move in.

"Why shouldn't you sit on it?" I cried. "Finish the sentence! Finish it!"

"'NEVER sit on the Gronk'—" Kelly read, her voice quivering.

"Ow!" I cried out as the Gronk pushed me

against the wall. "Read, Kelly! Read!" I was down on the floor. The Gronk rose up over me.

"'NEVER sit on the Gronk,'" Kelly started again, "'because . . . then it will want to sit on *you*!'"

SPLAT.

NUTCRACKER NIGHTMARE

"This must be a bad dream," I moaned.

My mom turned around and gave me a dirty look from the front seat of the car. "That's enough, Samantha," she snapped.

I hate when she calls me by my whole name. I waited until she turned around, then made a face at the back of her head.

My father glanced into the rearview mirror and caught me. "Sam!" he said. "We're not dragging you off to be tortured, you know. We're taking you to an exciting cultural event."

My dad is a college art professor. That means he's big on culture.

"I hope you'll be polite and thank Mrs. Boren for the tickets, Sam." My mom flipped down the visor to check her wavy brown hair in the mirror.

Mrs. Boren — or old Boring, as I call her — used to be my baby-sitter. She moved out of our neighborhood when I was eight, but I still remembered every horrible second I spent with her. She never let me do anything fun.

And now, four years later, she had found a new way to torture me. She was taking my family to the ballet for Christmas.

"I'm sure old Boring will love this stupid dress you made me wear." I pushed at the sleeves of the hideous, green taffeta dress, a hand-me-down from my oldest cousin. It was at least two sizes too big, with disgusting lacy bows on the shoulders.

"No name-calling, Samantha," my mom said sharply. "I loved *The Nutcracker* when I was your age," she added.

I couldn't help being grumpy. All my friends were going to the movies tonight and I was missing it.

I glanced at my wrist and realized I'd left my watch home. Just as well, I thought. I won't be able to count every endless second of ballet boredom.

I spotted Mrs. Boren as soon as we entered the lobby. She hadn't changed a bit. She was tall and chunky, with short black hair that seemed to be painted onto her head. Her clothes were dull black, her skin dull white. Only her huge gray eyes stood out. They seemed to see everything about you, even what you were thinking.

"Good evening, Samantha. I'm glad you came," she said.

"Uh, yeah," I mumbled. I wanted to be polite.

But old Boring's steely gaze was making me nervous.

My mom flashed me another dirty look. She and my dad chatted with old Boring as we walked through the lobby into the theater. I trailed behind them.

I took my seat on the aisle next to my mom. A tall woman was sitting in front of me. At first I thought she was wearing a big fur hat. Then I realized it was her hair. I wouldn't be able to see a thing without leaning way out over the aisle.

"Great," I muttered. "Just my luck."

Mom looked at me, then at the woman's tall, fuzzy hairdo. "Don't worry, Sam," she said. "I'm sure your father will switch seats with you."

Dad and Mrs. Boren turned to me. "Sure thing, Sam," Dad said, starting to get up.

I shuddered at the thought of sitting next to old Boring. "Forget it," I said hastily. "I'll stay here. At least dodging around for a view will give me something to do. It might even keep me awake."

I was sorry as soon as the words were out. My father frowned. My mother gasped. I glanced at Mrs. Boren, but she didn't seem upset at all.

"The girl hasn't learned to appreciate the ballet," she told my parents. "But she's young. These things take time. Lots and lots of time."

Mom looked ready to launch into another

round of scolding. I didn't wait around for it. "I'm going to the ladies' room," I said quickly. "I'll be right back."

There were several women in line. But by the time I came out, the theater lobby was empty.

Almost empty, that is.

"Hello, Samantha." Mrs. Boren was standing in the doorway.

"My name is Sam," I corrected her.

She didn't answer. That made me nervous.

"We'd better get going," I said. "The show must be about to start."

Her cold gray eyes stared at me. I started into the theater. "That means it's almost time to be bored to death," I muttered.

"Bored to death," Mrs. Boren repeated, her eyes narrowing. "I wonder if you know what boredom *really* is?"

I could feel my face turning red. I hadn't meant for her to hear that. "I don't know," I mumbled.

"It's time for you to learn some patience, Samantha." Mrs. Boren lifted her wrist and her sleeve fell back, revealing a strangely carved gold wristwatch. "Oh, yes, it's time."

She slowly tapped the watch three times with her right pointer finger. Then she turned and walked away without another word.

I returned to my seat just as the orchestra started to tune up.

"There you are," my mom said. "You were gone a long time."

"There was a line," I said. I didn't dare look at Mrs. Boren, who was back in her seat. All I wanted was to forget that freaky scene in the lobby.

My mind wandered to all the fun my friends were having without me. But that was too depressing. So I started thinking about the computer game my parents had given me for Christmas.

It was really complicated. So far, I'd never made it past Level Six. I thought about all the strategies I'd tried so far. Then I tried to figure out what I was doing wrong.

Maybe coming to the ballet hadn't been a total loss after all. It had given me plenty of time to think.

I heard a tuba blare out a few notes. Then a flute played a scale. "What's going on?" I whispered to my mom.

"They're warming up," she replied.

"Still?" I said in surprise. "They sure are taking long enough."

Mom rolled her eyes. "Be patient," she said. "The ballet will be starting soon."

The minutes crept by, one by one by one. The musicians continued tooting and trilling. After a while, my arm started to tingle. It had fallen asleep. I shook it out.

"Sam," Mom said sharply. "Sit still."

"Is this thing ever going to start?" I asked.

My mind drifted again. This time I couldn't help thinking about my friends. I wondered if they would go out for pizza after the movie. I wished I was with them. I even knew what I would have worn: the new rugby shirt my cousins gave me for Christmas.

That reminded me of my other gifts. To keep myself occupied, I listed them all in my head.

The orchestra went silent.

It's about time, I thought. I waited for the music to start. But several minutes passed in silence.

"What's happening?" I whispered finally.

"Ssssh." My mom's eyes were turned to the stage. She was smiling expectantly.

I leaned over to get a view past the hairdo. But the curtain stayed down. Finally, after what seemed like at least ten minutes, I caught movement out of the corner of my eye. I gazed toward the orchestra pit and saw the conductor lift his arms. The musicians slowly raised their instruments.

Still nothing happened. The conductor kept his arms raised. The orchestra kept their instruments ready. But nobody played a note.

What was going on? I glanced around and saw that the rest of the audience stared at the stage without moving.

I shifted in my seat, trying to get comfortable. Why hadn't this stupid ballet started yet?

The silence was eerie. Nobody shuffled in their seats, coughed, or whispered.

And my mom was still staring at the stage with that little smile on her face.

When the first note finally came, it startled me so much that my foot jerked forward and banged into the seat in front of me. The hairdo woman turned around and scowled.

The orchestra introduction was boring, so I stopped paying attention. Instead, I thought about the poem I was supposed to memorize for school. I knew most of it, but it was really long — twenty stanzas.

Reciting the poem in my head was actually sort of relaxing. But by the fifth time, I was definitely sick of it.

I peered around the hair in front of me. The music was still going, but the curtain was closed.

Hurray! I thought. I must have dozed off and missed the entire ballet. It seemed too good to be true.

"Is it ending?" I whispered.

"Very funny," my mom replied. "The dancing will start any minute now."

At first I thought she was teasing me, but I turned to the stage again and saw that the curtain was rising. It inched its way up. Several dancers were onstage, poised to begin.

How did I lose track of time like that?

I stifled a huge yawn. What time was it, anyway? I tried to see my mom's watch. But it was turned away from me.

Onstage, the dancers were moving slowly in their colorful tutus. They twirled around the stage, so slowly, as if in slow motion.

As they danced on and on, my left foot fell asleep. It felt as if pins and needles were being thrust right through my shoe. I stamped my foot hard, trying to get the circulation going.

That brought my mom out of her trance. "Quiet!" she whispered.

"But my foot's asleep," I protested.

I turned back to the stage. The dancers had left. The musicians were shuffling pages as they got ready for the next scene.

When it finally started, I gripped the arms of my seat and tried to pretend that everything was normal. But the dance went on and on.

It was taking forever!

I glanced over at my mom. She was smiling and humming under her breath as she watched the dancers moving so slowly across the stage. So slowly, they barely moved.

Something was wrong here. And I seemed to be the only one who knew it. But what could I do?

I closed my eyes and tried to think.

Suddenly the audience started to clap. That woke me from my thoughts. I joined in. The applause went on and on. After several minutes, I stopped clapping. But at a frown from my mom, I started again.

Ten minutes later, my hands were getting sore. I clapped as softly as I could.

Just when I was afraid my hands would start bleeding if I clapped any longer, the applause ended.

And another long pause came. The only sound was the musicians shuffling their scores.

The creepy silence lasted even longer this time. The audience sat still and waited.

Finally I couldn't take it anymore. "Mom," I whispered. My throat felt dry and scratchy. "What time is it?"

She sighed. "Honestly, Sam," she whispered back. "If you can't enjoy yourself, keep quiet so the rest of us can."

Mrs. Boren leaned forward so I could see her. "I know what time it is, Sam," she said. She held up her wrist with the strange watch on it. "It's time for you to learn some patience," she said. She tapped the watch.

My mother smiled. She didn't realize what Mrs. Boren was saying. But I did.

Mrs. Boren was responsible for this! She had cast some kind of spell over everyone to slow everything down. And now, hours and hours were passing as we sat here.

I had to do something. Who knew how long she

was planning to keep us trapped in this weird time warp!

I tried to move. For a second my limbs wouldn't obey. Finally they creaked to life, feeling stiff and cramped.

"Mom," I whispered urgently. "Listen. Something strange is going on here —"

She didn't let me finish.

"This is your last warning, Samantha," she whispered angrily. "One more word before this ballet is over, and you're grounded until *next* Christmas!"

But I hardly heard her. I had just taken a good look at her.

I gasped in horror.

It was dark in the theater, but there was no mistaking it. My mother's brown hair was streaked with patches of gray!

How long had we been sitting here?

I had to escape. Maybe once I was outside I could figure out how to save my family.

I stood and walked toward the exit, willing my rubbery legs to hurry. Why hadn't I done this earlier? Soon I would be outside in the fresh air. I would head straight for the police. Maybe they could save my parents and the rest of the audience from the old woman's curse — before it was too late.

But the exit didn't appear any closer. I sped up, breaking from a jog into a run. I ran until I was gasping for breath and there was a stitch in my side.

But no matter how fast my legs pumped, the lobby doors stayed where they were. When I turned around, my seat was only a few feet behind me.

With a defeated sigh, I walked back and collapsed into my chair.

Mrs. Boren leaned forward. "If you want to go to the snack bar, Samantha, it's closed while the performance is going on," she said sweetly. "You'll just have to be patient."

I glared at her. But I was too tired and scared to answer.

Suddenly I heard a loud *RRRRIP!* One of the seams in my dress had come apart. I stared down in surprise.

My sleeves were too short!

I had grown into — and out of — my cousin's dress while I was sitting here!

How long had it been? How long?

Finally, the curtain came down.

I sobbed out loud. I was so relieved. Yes! Now I could leave this nightmare ballet with my parents.

I started to stand up.

Mrs. Boren leaned forward again and smiled at me. "Be patient, Samantha," she said. "The first act is almost over. The second act will start *real* soon!"

THE ICE VAMPIRE

"Look! The judges are ready," Sam Weaver said. "I know our ice sculpture is going to win!"

"Sssh! Let's listen." His best friend, Billy Liff, elbowed him in the ribs.

The four judges strolled onto a wooden stage. It had been set up in the park for the Winter Carnival. Dozens of ice sculptures dotted the snow-covered lawn in front of the stage.

Sam brushed some ice shavings off the sculpture they had built. It was a huge, coiled cobra, ready to strike.

"And the winner is," one of the judges said into the microphone, "Ice Vampire, by Bram Stokeman."

"That stinks!" Billy said. He punched the cobra.

The judges climbed off the stage and made their way through the rows of sculptures. They reached the last row. One of them stuck a blue ribbon on the winning statue.

"Let's go check it out," Sam said. He and Billy pushed through the small crowd that had gathered behind the judges.

The winning statue was a very real-looking carving of a vampire. Fangs, cape, a long nose, and thin lips. Its eyes squinted. The blue ice gave it an eerie glow.

"Where did that one come from?" Billy asked.

"I don't know." Sam shrugged. "I didn't see it when we walked around before."

"We must have been too busy making ours to notice it," Billy said. "What a waste *that* was."

"A total waste," Sam groaned, kicking a clump of snow. "Want to go get some hot cider or something?"

The boys made their way across the park to the refreshment booth. They bought drinks and sat down at a picnic table.

"Hey! Sam! Billy! Who won?" It was Michelle Ahlberg, a girl from school.

"Some vampire statue," Sam grumbled. He crunched up his empty cider cup and tossed it into a trash barrel.

"Want to see our sculpture?" Billy asked Michelle.

"Sure!"

They raced back to the ice sculptures. "Check it out," Billy announced, pointing to the huge cobra.

Michelle let out a whistle. "Awesome," she said. She glanced around. "Where's the sculpture that won?"

Sam turned toward the last row, searching for the vampire. "That's weird," he muttered. "It's gone."

A sculpture of a girl stood in the spot where Sam swore the ice vampire had been. He gaped at the frozen sculpture. She looks exactly like my next-door neighbor, Sam realized. "Hey, you guys, doesn't that look like Rebecca Phillips?"

Billy and Michelle took a few steps closer and peered at the sculpture.

"Wow!" Billy exclaimed. "It does!"

Michelle giggled. "A Rebecca Phillips ice cube!"

Sam stared at the statue. There was something strange about it. It was carved as perfectly as the ice vampire had been. He could even see the statue's eyelashes and fingernails.

Sam gazed around the park. Where *did* the vampire sculpture go? Maybe I'm just looking in the wrong place, Sam told himself. It couldn't just disappear.

"It's getting cold out," Michelle said. "I'm going home." She waved good-bye and ran off.

Sam took another look at the Rebecca statue. The moon was up. Its light cast a white glow on the sculpture. The wind suddenly gusted, and the bare trees rustled and groaned.

"This place is creepy all of a sudden." Billy glanced around. "Everyone is gone. We should go too."

Sam couldn't take his eyes off the statue. It looked so *alive.*

"Come on, Sam," Billy insisted.

A low, eerie moan rang through the air.

Sam shivered. The boys turned around and started walking away.

"Ooooooohhhh." The moan rose up, louder this time.

The boys spun around. And stared at the frozen Rebecca sculpture. Its eyes seemed to be staring back at them. Pleading with them.

"Let's get out of here," Sam said.

The boys hurried along a row of statues. Sam felt a shiver run down his spine. He reached back to pull up his hood.

And a freezing-cold hand clamped down on his neck.

"Cut it out, Billy!" Sam cried.

He spun around. And gasped.

Towering over him stood the vampire ice sculpture!

Only it wasn't ice anymore.

The vampire had come alive.

Sam felt his heart slamming in his chest. He

rubbed his eyes. When he opened them, the vampire still stood there.

Sam backed up slowly. Billy grabbed Sam's arm and backed up too.

The creature grinned. His fangs glistened like tiny icicles. Patches of frost covered his sharp cheekbones. His eyes were dark and glassy — and had no pupils.

"Heat . . . ," the vampire murmured in a chilling whisper. He reached out one long, icy-clear hand. And grabbed Sam's wrist.

"Let go!" Sam screamed. The vampire's fingers gripped him tightly. Sam felt his skin grow cold. Icy needles shot up his arm. Suddenly, he couldn't feel his wrist anymore.

"Help!" Sam shrieked. "The vampire is turning me into ice!" Sam felt the cold creep into his chest. His lungs started to freeze! He couldn't breathe.

Sam punched at the vampire with his free arm. But the vampire didn't seem to notice. He stared into Sam's eyes. Sam felt himself getting colder . . . and suddenly sleepy. So sleepy.

"Let him go!" Billy screamed. He grabbed Sam around the waist. Billy tugged hard.

"Heat . . . ," the vampire moaned. He lost his grip on Sam's wrist. He snarled as Sam stumbled backward.

"Let's get out of here!" Billy yelled.

The boys raced through the row of statues. Behind them, the vampire's feet crunched over the snow.

"Heat . . . ," the vampire called after them.

The boys reached the street and ran toward Sam's house. They bolted inside and collapsed against the front door.

"We made it. We're safe," Sam gasped. He and Billy sat on the floor, taking deep breaths.

"He — he — he came to life," Billy stammered.

"Did he follow us?" Sam asked breathlessly.

They heard a scratching at the door.

Sam and Billy screamed. They whirled around.

"Heat . . . ," the vampire moaned from outside.

Sam and Billy jumped away from the door.

"Look!" Sam gasped. "The keyhole is frosting over!"

"I need heat," the vampire called. "Give me heat!" The doorknob rattled.

"Get out of here! Leave us alone!" Sam wailed.

Silence now.

The boys stared at the door.

Silence.

The keyhole was completely frozen over.

"Is he gone?" Sam whispered. "Is he gone for good?"

"Where is everybody?" Sam asked the next morning. He helped himself to cereal and milk.

"Your mom and dad are at the mall," Billy reported. Billy had slept over. "And Emily is out on the porch knocking down icicles."

Sam nodded. Emily is his older sister. He was supposed to help her pull the icicles down from the porch roof so they didn't fall on anyone. But he figured if he ate slowly, she'd be done when he got outside.

"Last night was so weird," Billy murmured.

"Did we really see an ice vampire last night?" Sam asked.

Billy shuddered. He'd had bad dreams all night. He still couldn't believe the ice sculpture had come to life and chased them.

He pushed Emily's mirror, hairbrush, and blow-dryer to one side of the table and set down his cereal bowl with a clunk.

"My sister thinks the kitchen is a beauty salon. And she *always* leaves her junk around," Sam complained. "Mom has a fit if I leave my sneakers on the table. But perfect Miss Emily gets away with —"

A terrified scream cut off Sam's words.

"That's Emily!" Sam shouted. He jumped up from his chair and raced to the kitchen window.

The ice vampire had returned. Blue veins sparkled under his clear skin. His cape rippled behind him. He grabbed Emily's hand!

Sam watched in horror as the creature held

Emily's hand tightly. A drop of water slid down the vampire's long nose. The frosty patches on his cheeks started to melt.

"He's pulling the heat from Emily!" Sam cried. "We have to save her!"

Sam flung open the back door. "Leave her alone!" he screamed. He pounced on the vampire. Billy yanked Emily free.

"Run!" Sam called. Billy and Emily escaped into the house.

The vampire spun around. He faced Sam.

"Heat . . . ," he moaned. "I need more heat." He stretched his icy hands toward Sam.

Sam's eyes landed on the icicles Emily had knocked to the ground. That's it! he thought. An icicle through the heart has to be the way to kill an ice vampire!

The vampire stepped closer. "Heat . . . give me your heat."

Sam snatched an icicle from the ground. He raised it high over his head.

The vampire flexed his icy, clear hands. He stepped forward.

"Yaaaa!" Sam screamed and stabbed the icicle into the vampire's chest. The blunt end broke off against the sculpture's icy body.

The vampire laughed. A cold, wet laugh.

Sam spun around and dove inside. He slammed the kitchen door and locked it.

Emily was standing by the kitchen table, rubbing her hands together. Her teeth were chattering, and her lips were blue.

"Did he leave?" she whispered.

"He's still out there," Sam told her. "I tried to kill him with an icicle, but he just laughed."

The vampire's face suddenly appeared at the kitchen window.

Emily shrieked and jumped away.

The vampire put his icy hands against the glass.

Sam watched in horror as the window frosted over. Then it cracked and shattered!

The vampire pushed the window frame in and stepped into the kitchen. "Heat . . . give me your *heat,*" he snarled.

Before the kids could move, the vampire swooped up to them. He grabbed Billy and dug his icy fingers into Billy's arm.

Billy let out a shriek. "He — he's *freezing* me!" Billy tried to pull loose.

"Heat . . . ," the vampire murmured, digging his icicle fingers deeper into Billy's warm flesh. "Yessss . . . heat . . ."

In a terrified panic, Sam grabbed the first thing he could find: Emily's portable blow-dryer. He suddenly had an idea.

"The battery is low," Emily warned. "I don't think it will work!"

But Sam clicked it on. The blow-dryer whirred loudly. Warm air flowed from its tip.

Sam aimed the dryer at the ice vampire's face.

At first, the creature didn't react. But then a strange smile spread over his clear, icy face. "Aaaaaaah." He uttered a moan and let go of Billy.

Billy stumbled away, rubbing his frozen arm.

"Ohhhhhhh," the vampire moaned again as the warm air poured over him. "Yesssss. Heat . . . so much heat . . ."

"He loves it!" Billy whispered.

"More . . . ," the vampire demanded. "Heat . . . more heat . . ."

Sam kept the whirring blow-dryer aimed at the grinning, sighing ice sculpture.

"This is awesome!" Sam declared, turning to Emily and Billy. "He won't freeze us now. He has all the heat he needs. Look how happy he is. Now he knows we're his friends. You know —"

"Uh . . . Sam?" Billy interrupted, shouting over the whir of the blow-dryer. "Sam?"

"What is it?" Sam replied.

"Turn around," Billy instructed. "There's one little problem."

"Huh?" Sam clicked off the blow-dryer and turned to the ice vampire. "Where is he?"

Billy pointed to the puddle on the floor. "You melted him."

All three of them stared in amazement at the big puddle. Then they began to laugh. And laugh.

And laugh. Sam slapped Billy on the back. Emily collapsed onto the floor in a fit of giggles.

Such wonderful laughter. The kind of laughter that comes when you know that you are finally safe from harm.

"That was so great!" Sam cried. He flicked on the blow-dryer and pointed it at Billy.

"I'm melting. I'm meeelting," Billy wailed. They all cracked up again.

The buzz of the blow-drier grew softer and softer. Then stopped.

"The batteries died," Emily said. "We're lucky that didn't happen a few minutes ago."

Crash!

"What was that?" Sam spun around.

A giant ice cobra slithered through the broken kitchen window.

"Whoooaah!" Billy uttered a shocked cry. "It — it's our sculpture! It's come to life too!"

"Hhhh-eat." The enormous snake flicked its hideous tongue. "Give me your heat — now!"

A HOLLY JOLLY HOLIDAY

The Krusher's giant body hurtled toward me. "Aaargh!" he growled. His muscles bulged. His face gleamed with sweat. His gigantic hands, each bigger than my head, formed into his famous, bone-crushing Monster Grip.

"Beth?" my older sister, Jody, called from the front hall. "Where are you?"

I reluctantly looked away from the wrestling match on TV. The Krusher had just locked his opponent, Gorgon, in the Monster Grip. The smaller wrestler struggled to get away.

"I'm in here," I called.

Jody appeared in the doorway of the den. She was still wearing her coat. My dog, Ivory, looked up from his spot in front of the fire. Then he lowered his head and went back to sleep.

"Guess what I found!" Jody said excitedly. She held up a shopping bag with Christmas bows all over it.

I shrugged. Jody and I might only be a year

apart in age. But we are decades apart when it comes to our personalities.

Why would I care what she had bought at the mall? Still, I decided I should try to look interested. After all, Christmas was next week. Maybe Jody was giving me a sneak preview of my present.

Jody opened the bag and pulled out a videotape. "Check it out!" She held it up.

I groaned when I recognized the picture on the box. "Oh, no. Not *Holly Jolly Holiday*!" It is Jody's favorite Christmas movie. It is also my *least* favorite. It is a silly, sappy story about the spirit of Christmas.

I hate everything about it. I especially hate its heroine. Susie Snowflake is nicer than Santa and more cheerful than the Easter Bunny. Truly sickening.

"Isn't it enough that it's on TV sixteen times a day?" I asked. "You can't possibly want to watch it more than that!"

Jody hugged the tape to her chest. "I could watch it *a hundred* times a day and never get tired of it," she said. "I'm just lucky I found it. The lady at The Christmas Shoppe said it's the only copy she's ever seen." Jody stepped forward to pop the tape into the VCR.

"Can't you watch later?" I cried. "*Wrestle-O-Rama* is on."

Jody glanced at the TV. The Krusher was getting ready to jump off the ropes onto Gorgon's head. My sister wrinkled her nose. She doesn't like wrestling. "Sorry," she said sweetly. "Mom said it's my turn."

I knew better than to argue. My mother had told me to turn off the TV an hour ago.

"You can stay and watch the movie with me if you want, Beth," Jody offered.

"I'd rather eat a reindeer," I muttered. But I had nothing better to do, so I stayed.

The tape started. Susie Snowflake danced out of the kitchen, tossing her shoulder-length red hair. "Christmas cookies to tempt your tummy!" she said cheerfully. "What are the magic words?" Her children squealed with delight. "Pretty-bitty please with Christmas trees!" they cried.

I groaned. I had almost forgotten how horrible this movie is. I watched as Susie Snowflake spread holiday cheer throughout her neighborhood. She danced. She sang. She baked dozens of cookies.

Then Susie visited a grumpy neighbor. She wanted to bring him the holiday spirit. She sang a geeky song about Christmas chuckles and Santa smiles. Then she moved in for the kill.

Her smile grew brighter. She tossed her red hair. She spread her arms. "Who can resist a holiday hug?" she chirped.

"I can!" I said, jumping up.

"Sssssh," Jody shushed me. Her eyes were glued to the screen.

I went upstairs to my room and pulled out the December issue of *Wrestle-O-Rama* magazine. The Krusher was on the cover, standing over a cowering opponent. Jody had given me a subscription last Christmas. I hope she is planning to renew it this year, I thought. I settled back to read.

The issue was packed with interesting articles. It took me a long time to read them all. By the time I finished, I noticed that a delicious smell was floating upstairs. I decided to investigate. It smelled as if Dad had started his holiday baking.

I tossed the magazine aside and ran downstairs. "Dad?" I called, rushing into the kitchen. Nobody was there. But several batches of Christmas cookies were cooling on the counter. I grabbed a star-shaped cookie. Still warm.

"Dad?" I called with my mouth full. I headed for the den. "Yo, Dad? Where are you?"

My mother and Jody glanced up from the TV. "Ssssh!" they said. They were watching *Holly Jolly Holiday*.

I rolled my eyes. I had been reading for at least a couple of hours. That meant they must have started the tape over again. I couldn't believe anybody would want to watch that movie even once, let alone twice in a row.

"Where's Dad?" I asked. "I want to tell him his cookies are awesome."

"He's out in the garage," my mother replied, "but he didn't make the cookies. I did."

"*You* made them?" I said. Then I laughed. My mother doesn't bake. She never goes near the kitchen if she can help it. The only thing she ever makes is toast. And she even burns that half the time.

"You're kidding, right?" I said.

My mother smiled. "I know I don't usually like to bake. But I was watching this lovely movie with your sister and I suddenly had the urge to make some Christmas cookies to tempt your tummy."

I couldn't believe what my mother was saying. What was even weirder was the sound of her voice. Then I suddenly realized who she sounded like. She sounded like Susie Snowflake!

I glanced at the screen, where Susie was tap-dancing with Santa. "Very funny, Mom," I said. This was obviously some kind of joke. Jody had probably put Mom up to it because she knew I hated *Holly Jolly Holiday*.

Before I could say anything else, I noticed something that made my jaw drop. My mother's blond hair had turned light red!

"What did you do to your hair?" I asked. Then I glanced at Jody. Her waist-length hair was even redder than our mother's. Ivory looked up from his spot by the roaring fire. He let out a little bark. I looked at my dog and frowned. His white fur had a pinkish tinge.

"What's going on here?" I asked.

"What do you mean, dearie?" my mother asked.

"Huh?" Mom never calls me "dearie." Susie Snowflake calls people "dearie."

"This isn't funny anymore," I said.

Mom didn't reply. Instead, she and Jody started singing along to the tape. "'Where Santas dance and children play, it's a Holly Jolly Holiday . . .'"

I couldn't take it anymore. I hurried out of the room. My mother and my sister were acting really weird. They probably thought it was funny, but I didn't. Not at all.

I paused outside the den. I had just caught my reflection in the hall mirror. My dark blond hair had a slight reddish tint!

I stared at myself. My heart started pounding as I tried to think of an explanation. Was there a chemical leak in the house that was affecting everybody's hair color? Was something wrong with my eyes?

I had to figure out what was going on.

I found my father in his garage workshop. He was working on Jody's Christmas gift, a fancy jewelry box. "Hi, BB," he said. That is his nickname for me.

"Dad, check out my hair," I said. "Notice anything?"

He took a close look. "It looks red," he said. "Did you color it?"

"No." I told him the whole story. "At first I thought Jody and Mom were playing a joke on me," I finished. "But now I think it's more serious than that."

"A joke, huh?" Dad said, frowning. "It sounds as if you're playing a joke — on your old dad." He stroked his thick black beard. "Okay. What's the punch line?"

"I'm serious," I insisted. "Go inside and see for yourself. Their hair is redder than mine."

My father sighed and set down his tools. "Fine," he said. "I can tell you aren't going to give me any peace until I go look."

I perched on a stool and waited for him to return. I was still scared, but I felt better now that Dad was on the case. I knew he didn't believe me — but he would.

I waited for ten minutes, then fifteen. It was chilly in the workshop. What was keeping him?

Finally I gave up and went inside. "Dad?" I called.

"In here, dearie," he called back from the den.

Dearie? I thought in dismay. Oh, no!

I went into the den. The first thing I saw was the TV. The last scene of *Holly Jolly Holiday* was playing. My mother and sister were sitting on the couch. I gasped when I saw them.

My mother's hair was shoulder-length and shiny red. The ends flipped up, just like Susie Snowflake's. Jody's hair looked exactly the same!

I turned to my father for help. But I almost screamed when I saw him. His normally black hair was now almost as red as Mom's. And his beard and mustache were gone!

"Dad! Did you shave?" I asked. I didn't expect an answer. I glanced at Ivory and saw that his fur was almost the same shade of red as Mom's and Jody's hair.

Somehow, my whole family was turning into Susie Snowflake!

"Don't fret, dearie," my dad said with a smile. He pointed to a platter on the coffee table. "Have some Christmas cookies to tempt your tummy."

I almost reached for one. When I realized what I was doing, I jerked my hand back. This was no time for a snack.

"Oh, dearie me!" I cried.

I gasped as I realized what I had just said. That scared me more than all the rest put together. I was changing too!

I glanced into the mirror over the fireplace. Sure enough, my hair was redder now. It was also an inch or two longer than its usual chin length. The ends were starting to flip up.

It was the movie. It had to be! That stupid Susie Snowflake movie was changing all of us. Maybe it isn't too late, I thought. The movie was ending. Jody got up and went to the VCR.

"Out of my way, dearie," I said. "Uh, I mean, Jody. I need that videotape."

Jody paused with her finger on the rewind button. "Is something wrong, dearie?"

"Stop calling me that!" I snapped. "Something is wrong — really wrong. And it has to do with that tape. Give it to me."

Jody ejected the tape. But instead of handing it over, she stuck it behind her back. "What are the magic words?" she asked in a lilting Susie Snowflake voice.

I gritted my teeth. "Please," I said.

My sister shook her head. My parents smiled. "That's not it," Jody sang out. She giggled and waggled one finger. "You have to know the right magic words, dearie. Otherwise you'll just have to wait until Santa's at the gate."

That was another line from *Holly Jolly Holiday*. "Shut up!" I cried. "Don't you see what's happening? Anybody who watches that videotape starts turning into Susie Snowflake! We have to destroy it before it's too late."

My family stared at me blankly. Even Ivory gave me a blank look.

"What are the magic words?" Jody repeated cheerfully.

I took a deep breath and tried to calm down. What was that sappy line from the movie? If I could remember it, Jody might actually hand over the tape.

"Uh, pretty please with a cherry on top?" I said.

Jody shook her head.

"Please with a holiday hug?" I tried.

Jody shook her head again.

I had been forced to watch that stupid movie often enough. Why couldn't I remember the line?

"Oh, sugar cookies!" I said. It wasn't what I had meant to say at all.

There was only one thing to do. It was risky, but I had no choice.

Susie Snowflake knew the magic words. If I let myself fall deeper under the spell, I could remember the words. And then I could get the tape.

I only hoped I could pull myself back out in time. Otherwise, I'd end up being a Susie Snowflake look-alike forever!

I tried to relax. I hummed a few bars of the movie theme song. I grabbed a cookie and nibbled on it. Before long, I could feel the corners of my mouth turning up in a big, bright smile. I bent down to pat Ivory's furry red head.

I started to sing. "'Where Santas dance in bright red pants . . .'"

Visions of sugarplums danced through my head. I had a sudden urge to bake some cookies.

Maybe I was making too much of all this, I

thought. What is wrong with a little holly jolly holiday spirit, after all?

Words drifted through my head. Happy words. Christmas words. One sentence in particular. For some reason, it seemed important. But I couldn't remember why.

I turned to Jody. Her pretty red hair was flipped up at the ends. She was smiling.

I smiled back and said the words that were still dancing through my head: "'Pretty-bitty please with Christmas trees!'"

"That's it!" Jody shoved the videotape into my hands. I stared at it. *Holly Jolly Holiday*. What a lovely movie! It would be the perfect thing to watch right now.

And I loved Susie Snowflake. She was everything I ever wanted to be.

I took a step toward the VCR. Something was playing quietly on the TV. I squinted at it. Dearie me, what were those large men doing? Why were they trying to hurt each other?

One of the men looked very familiar. "The Krusher?" I murmured.

My real thoughts suddenly came flooding back. They were all tangled and confused with Susie Snowflake's cheerful Christmas thoughts. But I knew what I had to do.

"Aaargh!" I shouted, just like the Krusher.

I turned and threw the videotape into the roaring fire.

My family screamed as the tape went up in flames. Ivory barked wildly.

As the tape burned, all my urges to talk and act and think like Susie Snowflake melted away. Ivory whined and shoved his cold nose into my hand. When I looked down at him, I saw that his red fur was already fading back to white.

The whole family gathered in the den on Christmas Eve. Everything seemed normal. Everyone's hair was its usual color. My father's beard was as thick as ever.

Mom hadn't been near the kitchen in days. And Jody was the only one humming the *Holly Jolly Holiday* theme song — which actually *was* normal.

We hadn't talked about what had happened the week before.

"Open this one next," Jody urged. She handed me a gift wrapped in red-and-green paper. "I know you're going to love it."

I ripped open the package eagerly. I gasped when I saw what was inside. "Oh, wow!" I cried. "Thanks, Jody!"

It was a tape starring the Krusher. I popped it into the VCR. "*Wrestle-O-Rama* presents the Krusher in some of his greatest matches!" an announcer said.

Then the Krusher appeared on the screen,

looking as mean and dangerous as always. “Aaaargh!” he screamed with rage.

I grinned with excitement. This was the best Christmas present ever! “Where did you find it?” I asked Jody. “I didn’t know the Krusher had his own video.”

“I know,” Jody replied. “The lady at The Christmas Shoppe said it’s the only copy she’s ever seen.”

WHY I HATE JACK FROST

I gazed out the front window of our new house in Arizona. There were no trees in the yard. No drifts of snow. No ice. Instead, I saw only sand and cactus. Tall, green, prickly, ugly cactus.

Instead of a green Christmas wreath, a circle of red chilies hung on our door. Instead of gray clouds sprinkling snowflakes, a bright blue sky. A warm yellow sun shone over everything.

"I hate winter here!" I cried aloud.

"Of course you do, Jared," Mom called from the other room. "You're twelve, and you've always lived somewhere that has snowy winters. You have to give the desert a chance. You'll learn to love it."

No way, I thought.

"Look on the bright side," Mom said. "Back home, you couldn't ride your bike during Christmas vacation."

"I'd rather ride my sled," I muttered.

Still, riding my bike sounded like a good idea.

It might take my mind off how homesick I felt. "I'm going out for a while," I called.

"Good!" Mom replied. "Just be back before dinner. We're going to trim the tree this evening."

Tree. Hah. I glanced at the green plastic tree in the living room. Like everything else in this desert winter, our Christmas tree was fake.

My bike stood propped against the front wall of the house. Glancing around, I thought that even the houses looked wrong. My house and all the others in our new neighborhood are pale pink. All of them have flat roofs. They look like ugly shoe boxes.

I pedaled to the mall. I chained my bike, then went inside. Christmas music blared from loudspeakers. People crowded the walkways. Everyone was smiling. Everyone seemed to be full of Christmas spirit.

Everyone but me.

I wanted to see shoppers bundled up in heavy coats and jackets. But everyone wore shorts and T-shirts. It didn't feel like Christmas. It felt more like the Fourth of July!

And then I saw it.

A tall green fir tree stood in the center of the mall.

It looked just like the Christmas trees we used to decorate back home.

I raced toward it. A spicy scent filled the air. The tree was real. It was decorated with hundreds of beautiful, old-fashioned ornaments. A small sign said that the ornaments were for sale.

I'll buy one! I thought. That will make it seem more like a real Christmas.

I spotted a large ornament shaped like an old-fashioned house. The house had white wooden walls and a slanted roof. The roof was covered with snow. A tiny elf stood in the doorway of the house. He wore a green suit and a red scarf.

"You like it?" a voice cracked in my ear.

I glanced up. A very old man stood beside me. "I can see you miss real winter," the old man said. "These ornaments are the next best thing. The one you're looking at is very special. It's the home of Jack Frost, who brings the ice."

I reached up to touch the ornament. It felt cold! I wondered if it had been kept in the refrigerator or something. "I'll take it!" I exclaimed.

I paid the old man, shoved the ornament in my backpack, and sped home. I couldn't wait to hang the ornament on our tree.

But as soon as I caught sight of the ugly tree in our living room, I changed my mind. The ornament was much too good for a fake tree.

Instead, I decided to hang Jack Frost and his house above my bed. That way, I could bring a little bit of real winter into my room.

The next morning, I gazed out the window. I couldn't believe my eyes. Everything was covered in white. A real snowstorm! The flakes were so thick, the air looked white. The wind blew drifts across the yard.

Quickly, I dug through my closet for my parka. Then I ran outside. I began rolling snow for a snowman. What fun!

When the body was built, I shoved broomsticks in the snowman's sides for arms. Then I put chunks of coal on the head to make eyes, nose, and a mouth. Finally, I placed a stocking cap on the snowman's head.

"Good job!" cried a cheerful voice. I turned to see an elf, dressed all in green. He had a red beard. A long red scarf hung around his neck. He looked exactly like Jack Frost in the ornament I'd bought!

Jack Frost snapped his fingers — and the snowman's eyes blinked!

"Ahhh! That feels good," the snowman said in a rumbling, deep voice. He raised his arms up and down. Then he turned to me.

"Race you to the pond!" he rumbled. He waddled off over a hill. I raced after him.

On the other side of the hill was a beautiful, gleaming, icy pond. A pair of ice skates sat on the bank of the pond. They were exactly my size. I put on the skates and began to glide out over the frozen water.

The snowman skated beside me. We skated

faster and faster. I could feel the icy wind biting my face, and it was great! I was back in winter!

The snowman and I skated to the other side of the pond. We began making snowballs and throwing them at Jack Frost. The snowballs flew faster and faster.

After a while, my teeth were chattering. "I th-th-think it's time to stop!" I stammered.

The snowman and Jack Frost vanished in a spray of snow.

I opened my eyes. And lifted my head from my pillow. I'd been dreaming. I glanced over at my new Christmas tree ornament. Jack Frost grinned down from his little house.

All day, I thought about the dream. It had seemed so real!

Thinking about skating on the icy pond made me shiver. I couldn't seem to get warm. I changed out of my shorts and put on jeans and a sweater.

After breakfast, Tim, my friend who lives next door, came over. "Come on, Jared," he said. "Let's go for a bike ride."

"I don't think so," I replied. "It's too cold. I think I'll stay inside." I curled up next to the window with the sunlight streaming in. But the golden rays felt cold, as cold as ice.

That night, I was so cold, I went to bed early. I piled on extra blankets to try to warm up.

As soon as my eyes closed, Jack Frost greeted me. "Welcome back to real winter, Jared!" he exclaimed. I gasped when I saw that instead of fingernails, the elf had sharp, blue icicles at the ends of his fingers. "Let's go sledding!"

I followed Jack Frost up a long, slick hill. The wind blew even harder than it had in the first dream. I shivered. At the top of the hill stood a bright red sled. I climbed on behind Jack Frost. I was shivering so hard, I could barely hold on to him.

"Let's go!" the elf cried.

The sled raced down the hill. Faster and faster it sped. The cold wind whistled by my face. I could feel my cheeks freezing. The sled zigged and zagged along the steep slope.

I held on as tightly as I could. I stared ahead. The sled headed toward the edge of a cliff. Faster and faster.

My heart began to pound.

"Stop!" I shouted. "Stop!"

I woke up. Late-morning sun streamed in the window. But my face felt damp and cold. My teeth chattered.

I glanced at the ornament of Jack Frost above my bed.

I felt a shiver go down my back. Just looking at the ornament made me feel colder.

I opened the closet and dug through a trunk of

clothes from back home. I put on my long johns under my jeans, then a long-sleeved shirt, then a sweater, then a sweatshirt. I still felt so cold, I could barely move my fingers.

I pulled the ornament off my bedpost. I didn't want it in my room anymore. I took it downstairs and hung it on the tree in the living room.

"What a lovely ornament!" my mother exclaimed.

"It's Jack Frost," I told her.

She narrowed her eyes at me.

"Speaking of Jack Frost, why are you wearing all those clothes?"

"I'm freezing cold!" I told her.

"Cold?" she replied. "How can you be cold? It's seventy degrees today!" She placed her hand on my forehead. "You don't seem to have a fever," she said. "But you'd better stay inside, just in case."

I spent the day in my room watching TV, drinking hot soup, covered up with blankets.

I decided Mom was right. I must be sick. That was why I felt so cold. All I needed to get well, I thought, was a good night's sleep.

"Come on, Jared! Let's make snow angels!" Jack Frost greeted me. I couldn't believe I was having another winter dream!

I followed the elf out into the snow. Jack Frost pushed me down into the wet, deep slush. "Move your arms in circles," he told me. "Make angel wings."

My arms kept moving back and forth in the snow. And now I realized I was sinking *into* the snow. I gazed up. Jack Frost stood a long way above. Walls of snow rose on all sides of me as I sank deeper and deeper.

I struggled to sit up. But the more I struggled, the deeper I sank, and the colder I felt.

I watched in horror as Jack Frost tossed a shovel of snow on top of me. The snow hit my face hard and covered my eyes. I was being buried alive! Buried alive in a grave of snow!

When I woke up, it was morning. Bright sunshine shone through my bedroom window. I reached over to touch the window glass. It was as cold as an ice cube.

Shivering, I dressed in all my winter clothes. Then I put on my heavy parka and knit cap and went downstairs.

The ornament of Jack Frost glittered from the family Christmas tree. I yanked it off the tree and stuffed it in my pocket. I hurried out through the backyard. The cactus baked under the yellow sun. But I couldn't feel any of the warmth. I felt only chill, all the way through my body.

I stepped out to the alley. I pulled the lid off the trash can and jammed the ornament into it, way down deep with rotting orange peels and egg-shells.

"That's that!" I said out loud. "So long, Jack Frost!"

That night, my parents and I stayed up late wrapping Christmas packages. I felt so cold, I kept my mittens on. I was shivering so hard, I didn't think I'd be able to fall asleep.

But the second I closed my eyes, Jack Frost was back.

"Come on, Jared," the elf urged. "Let's go play in the snow."

"No!" I shouted. "I don't want to! Leave me alone!"

"No way!" Jack Frost exclaimed. He grabbed my hands. The skin on my hands froze to his. I had to follow him out to the cold, snowy field.

The snowman I'd built was there, inside a snow fort. "Come on, Jared!" it cried. "Let's play in the snow!"

No, I thought. *I won't!* But I felt myself climb into the snow fort. We had an endless snowball fight.

After a while, I felt so sleepy, I could barely move. "I want to go to sleep," I told Jack Frost.

"You can nap in my house," Jack Frost told me.

He led me across the snowy field. Under a big tree stood a familiar-looking, old-fashioned house. I realized it was Jack Frost's house from the ornament!

In front of the house stood a small Christmas tree.

I started for the door of the house.

"Not so fast!" Jack Frost stopped me. "First you must help me decorate my tree."

"What do you mean?" I asked.

He led the way behind the house, to an alley. A familiar-looking alley. The alley behind my own house.

"Go on, Jared," Jack Frost said sternly. "Get the ornament out of the trash can."

"If you don't, you'll get even colder," he warned.

I felt so cold — and so sleepy. I pulled off the lid and reached deep into the frozen trash. I found the ornament and picked it up. Then I followed Jack Frost to the front of his little house.

"Hang it on the tree, Jared," he ordered.

I hung the ornament on the tree. The door to Jack Frost's home sprang open. I entered. It was small and tidy inside. A fire burned in the fireplace. But it gave off no warmth. I didn't care. I was so sleepy. I curled up in front of the fire and fell asleep.

Warm sun beat down on my back. I glanced up at the blue sky. I was in the backyard of my house in Arizona. For some reason I was dressed in layers and layers of clothes.

The fierce sun beat down on me. Sweat poured down my face. I took off the parka, the sweater, the long johns. I stripped down to my bathing trunks.

But it didn't help. I ran to the next-door neighbors' house. The clear water in their pool looked cool and inviting. I took a running start and jumped in.

But the water wasn't cool.

It was boiling hot!

And then I realized that this was all part of a new dream.

Wake up, I told myself. *Wake up now.*

When I opened my eyes, the swimming pool was gone. The hot, steaming water was gone.

I was back in Jack Frost's little house.

Icicles hung from the windows — on the inside.

It was cold, so cold.

Jack Frost entered the room. "Good morning, Jared," he said. "I heard you cry out in your sleep. Did you have a bad dream?"

"Huh?" I sat up, feeling dazed. "*You're* the bad dream!" I cried. "I'm dreaming now! And when I wake up, I'm going to be in my nice warm bed in my new pink house in hot, sunny Arizona!"

The elf twisted his face in confusion. "Arizona? Do you really think you live in Arizona?"

"Of course I do!" I screamed. "And when I wake up —"

He didn't let me finish. He pulled me outside. The ground lay covered with snow. And heavy flakes were coming down.

"This is where you live, Jared," Jack Frost said softly.

"No!" I shrieked. "Noooooo! I'm dreaming! I know I am! I'm —"

I stopped because something on Jack Frost's Christmas tree caught my eye.

The ornament.

The glass ornament.

I stepped up to it. Pulled it close — and gasped in horror.

Inside the ornament, under a blazing sun, stood a little pink house surrounded by cactus plants.

"That's my house!" I wailed. "My house in the desert!"

Jack Frost gently wiped snow off my shoulder. "Poor guy," he murmured. "That ornament must have given you nightmares. You live here. With me. Now get dressed and we'll have a nice, long snowball fight."

MARSHMALLOW SURPRISE

"Faster! Faster!" Marsha Zane shrieked.

Her sled streaked across the snow. She let out a whoop and plunged down the icy slope of Spooner Hill.

Her brothers, Ricky and Ronnie, zoomed past her.

"Out of our way, slowpoke!" Ricky hooted.

"Coming through!" Ronnie yelled.

Their sleds sprayed snow in Marsha's face.

"I'll get you geeks!" she shouted. The snow tickled her face as she soared after the boys.

Marsha is twelve — and she wasn't about to let a nine-year-old terror and an eight-year-old menace beat her in a sled race. No way!

She steered her sled around a sharp curve. The freezing wind made her eyes water. But she was catching up! She blinked hard and stared down at the bottom of the hill.

Oh, no.

"Look out!" she screamed at the boys. "We're heading right for Mrs. Spooner's yard!"

Too late.

"I can't stop!" Ricky bellowed.

The boys and Marsha hurtled past Mrs. Spooner's big NO TRESPASSING sign. Their sleds leaped over a huge pile of snow and soared through the air — into Mrs. Spooner's garden.

Ricky's sled landed in a thorny rosebush. He howled in pain.

Then Ronnie's sled skidded and flipped onto a frozen shrub. Ronnie tumbled to the ground with a loud grunt.

Marsha's sled plowed through the middle of the garden. It flew over frozen flower beds and icy branches.

Nothing could stop it.

Except Mrs. Spooner's mailbox!

Marsha screamed. Her sled crashed into the wooden post of the mailbox. The post cracked. Marsha slid forward, and — *WHAM!* Her head slammed the wooden post.

"Whoooa!" Marsha moaned. She rubbed her head. Then she gazed up at the tall white mailbox — just in time to watch it tilt to one side. And crash to the ground.

Ricky and Ronnie stood up and brushed themselves off.

"Are you okay, Marsha?" Ricky called.

Marsha sat up. She could feel a bump already

swelling under her short blond hair. "I guess," she mumbled.

"Yeah, but look at the mailbox," Ronnie pointed out. "Wait until Mrs. Spooner sees that. You're dead meat, Marsha."

Marsha studied the broken mailbox. The wooden post was cracked, and the white metal was crunched. It was completely destroyed.

Marsha's stomach twisted into a knot. "Maybe I can offer to pay for it," she muttered nervously.

"Yeah, right. You know Mrs. Spooner is going to get you now," Ricky said. "Remember the time she called the police because Sparky dug up her garden?"

"Forget that," Ronnie added. "Remember the time she called Dad just because we cut across the corner of her yard on the way to school?"

Marsha began to tremble. The wind felt colder than before.

"You know what a kid told me?" Ricky whispered. "He said he heard that Mrs. Spooner buries kids in her garden!"

"That's so stupid," Marsha scoffed. "She's not going to hurt us. She's just mean, that's all."

"That's why it's so much fun playing tricks on her," Ricky said. "She gets really crazy!"

"My favorite is ringing her doorbell and running away," Ronnie said, grinning.

Marsha frowned. "Well, that's probably why

Mrs. Spooner is so mean. Let's at least apologize for knocking over her mailbox."

The boys gasped.

"No way!" Ricky sputtered. "Let's get out of here! Now!"

"Yeah, before she catches us!" Ronnie added.

The boys grabbed Marsha by the arms. They turned around — and gasped.

The path was blocked — by Mrs. Spooner!

The tall, skinny woman stared down at the kids. Her long white hair was twisted high in a bun. Her thin lips were pressed together. The skin around her yellow-brown eyes was crinkled like old newspaper.

"Good day for sled-riding!" Mrs. Spooner chuckled.

"Huh?" Marsha couldn't believe it.

Mrs. Spooner was actually smiling!

The old woman glanced down at the broken mailbox. Marsha's heart sank.

"I see you've had an accident," Mrs. Spooner said softly. "I hope nobody was hurt."

Marsha rubbed her head. "I have a little bump," she replied. "Don't worry, I'm okay. But your mailbox is ruined."

Mrs. Spooner shook her head. "Oh, that can be fixed," she said. "As long as you children are all right. You must be cold!"

The boys shivered and stood closer to Marsha.

The icy wind was starting to make their teeth chatter.

"I know just what you need," Mrs. Spooner suggested. "A big cup of my special hot cocoa! Do you boys like hot cocoa?"

Ricky and Ronnie glanced nervously at each other.

"Um, no thanks. We don't want to put you to any trouble," Marsha said. She glanced up at the sky. Evening had turned everything gray. A pale, full moon was rising behind the bare trees.

"No trouble at all!" the old woman said. "Come right inside! I *insist*."

Mrs. Spooner turned and stepped onto the front porch. Marsha followed behind her.

Ricky grabbed Marsha's arm. "Are you crazy?" he whispered. "It's a trick!"

"I don't want to go in there," Ronnie cried.

Marsha yanked their arms. "Come on. We can't say no. It's not polite."

The boys gazed fearfully at the big old house. Marsha marched to the front door. Ricky and Ronnie followed slowly.

"Come in! Come in!" Mrs. Spooner beckoned.

They stepped into a large entry hall with flowered wallpaper. Marsha gazed around. Mrs. Spooner had lived here forever, but Marsha had never been inside.

Glowing candles on the wall cast eerie shadows. All of the doors off the hall were shut.

Marsha pulled off her ski parka, and snow dripped onto the floor. The boys tried to wipe their big rubber boots on the mat, but they tracked slush into the hall.

Mrs. Spooner scowled. Then she caught Marsha's eye and broke into a smile.

"That can be wiped right up," she said. "I haven't had company in so long. What's a little mess?"

The kids turned to follow Mrs. Spooner down the hall. The front door slammed behind them with a loud *BANG*!

Marsha yelped and the boys spun around.

Mrs. Spooner laughed. "It's the wind," she explained. "These old houses are so drafty."

Marsha shivered.

"Come inside and sit in the kitchen, where it's warm," Mrs. Spooner offered. She turned and led the children to the end of the hall. She pushed open a creaky wooden door.

Marsha gasped. The kitchen shelves were crammed with thousands of bottles and jars. Dried plants and flowers hung thickly from the ceiling. A fire crackled and hissed in a big black stove in the corner. The room was bursting with strange and spicy aromas.

Marsha stepped inside and gazed around nervously.

What's in all of those jars? she wondered.

She looked closer. The glass canning jars were filled with grains and seeds and roots and berries — and lots of weird stuff Marsha couldn't identify. She leaned forward to study a jar.

Her heart stopped.

Were those *eyeballs* in that jar?

Human eyeballs!

She opened her mouth to scream, but stopped. She stared at the jar again.

No. Not eyeballs. Small white onions.

Relax, Marsha, she told herself. You're acting as stupid as your brothers!

"Sit down! Sit down!" Mrs. Spooner insisted. "Warm yourselves by the stove. I'll spoon up some of my special hot cocoa."

Ricky and Ronnie plopped themselves down on two rocking chairs next to the stove. Marsha sat at the table.

Mrs. Spooner dipped a ladle into a gigantic bubbling pot and stirred. "It's an old family recipe," she said. "It has a secret ingredient — a special herb from my garden. My cocoa even has a secret name."

"Really? What's its name?" Marsha asked.

Mrs. Spooner smiled and winked. "Marshmallow Surprise," she said quietly.

The old woman ladled out three cups of hot cocoa.

That pot is so big! Marsha thought. She must have enough cocoa for every kid in town!

Mrs. Spooner handed a cup to each of the boys, then to Marsha. "Here you go!" she said.

"Thank you," Marsha said politely.

The rich smell of chocolate filled Marsha's nose. The boys raised the cups to their mouths and gulped.

"Excellent," Ricky said.

"Awesome!" Ronnie agreed.

Marsha sipped the rich chocolate and grinned. "It's so good, Mrs. Spooner," she said. "But where are the marshmallows?"

A smile spread across Mrs. Spooner's face. "You'll see," she said mysteriously. "Drink up! Drink up!"

Ricky and Ronnie gulped their cocoa down. Marsha sipped hers slowly.

"My family has never given the secret recipe away," Mrs. Spooner said.

Ricky glanced up from his cup. "Why?" he asked.

Mrs. Spooner smiled at him. "You'll see!"

The old woman flung open the door of the old black stove. The fire crackled gently.

She tossed a log on. The fire roared up, snapping and blazing.

"Mrs. Spooner," Marsha said, "it's really nice of you to make us cocoa. But it's getting dark out. We really have to go."

"Yeah. Thanks," Ricky said.

"Oh, it's nothing," Mrs. Spooner replied with a sly grin. "I'm just paying you back. Paying you back for all the neighborly things you've done for me."

Marsha cleared her throat. "Neighborly things, Mrs. Spooner?" she asked nervously. "What neighborly things?"

The white-haired woman slammed the stove door. She spun around and stared hard at the children. Mrs. Spooner pointed a long, bony finger at Ricky. "Let's see. You hit a baseball through my window last summer, Ricky," she said.

Ricky stammered and nodded.

Mrs. Spooner pointed at the other boy. "And you smashed your bicycle into my fence last fall, Ronnie."

Then Mrs. Spooner turned to Marsha. "And you, Marsha!" she exclaimed. "You destroyed my mailbox today! And I'm sure you were going to run off and leave it there. Just as your brothers did after they broke my window and my fence."

Marsha suddenly felt sick. Mrs. Spooner had only pretended to be friendly to get them into her house. She had tricked them!

"We really have to leave," she told the old woman. Marsha's eyes turned to the window. Dark outside now. A full moon hung over the bare trees.

"Yes. We have to go — now!" Ronnie insisted.

"We're warning you —!" Ricky cried shrilly. "You have to let us go!"

Mrs. Spooner's cruel smile spread over her face. "You can't," she murmured.

"But — why not?" Marsha cried in a trembling voice.

"Because of the Marshmallow Surprise," Mrs. Spooner replied, her eyes flashing excitedly. "I put a special ingredient in your cocoa. Do you feel your bones starting to soften? Do you feel your bodies turning to mush?"

"But — but —" Ricky gasped.

"The cocoa will turn *you* into marshmallows," Mrs. Spooner cackled gleefully. "Do you understand? *You* are the Marshmallow Surprise!"

The old woman crossed her arms in front of her chest and waited patiently for the three kids to turn to mush.

Marsha and the two boys stood up. And turned to her slowly.

And as they turned, their bodies began to change.

"We warned you to let us go," Marsha said.

"But you didn't listen to us," Ronnie murmured.

"So now," Ricky added, "we have a surprise for you."

Marsha uttered a low growl as her fangs slid

down over her chin. Thick brown wolf fur sprouted over her face, her arms, her entire body.

The boys raised their wolf snouts to the full moon and opened their fanged mouths in long howls.

"You — you are werewolves!" Mrs. Spooner shrieked.

Her last words.

The three roaring wolves opened their fangs hungrily — and pounced.

"Marshmallow Surprise," Marsha growled.

"Yummm!" the boys exclaimed.

MONSTER ON THE ICE

The minute I walked into my room, I heard it. There was someone in my closet.

I crept to the closet door. I took a deep breath and yanked it open. "Gotcha!" I shouted.

"Yaaiii!" my little sister, Jessica, shrieked.

I grabbed her arm and dragged her out of the closet.

"Max! You scared me," she whined. She yanked her arm out of my grip.

"Yeah, well, you're going to be superscared if I catch you messing with my stuff again," I told her.

Jessica is always snooping around in my things. Mom tells me to be patient, she's only six, blah, blah, blah. But tripping over my little sister every time I turn around is a major drag.

What's worse is everyone always says how we look alike. I don't see it. So what if we both have brown hair and blue eyes? A ton of people do.

Jessica is a wimpy little girl. I'm a boy! I'm

twelve and I'm an athlete. I won MVP two seasons in a row for my hockey team.

"What were you doing in there?" I demanded.

"I just wanted to borrow some of your clothes," Jessica said.

I stared down at her. "My clothes won't fit you," I said. As if I needed to point that out!

"Not for me. For Stinker!"

I stared at her. "Jessica, if you put my clothes on Stinker, you're in big trouble." Stinker is our German shepherd.

Jessica pouted. "He would look cool."

I pushed Jessica out of the room and followed her into the hall. I shut my bedroom door. "Don't go in there again," I ordered her.

I walked back down to the kitchen. Mitch Bowen and Steve Bell from my hockey team sat at the table, gobbling cookies. Steve is my best friend.

"Hey, guys," I announced. "She was up there all right. She wanted to put my clothes on the dog!"

"Awwww! That's so cute," Mitch said in a high voice.

We all laughed.

I reached under the table and patted Stinker. "Don't worry, Stink," I said. "I won't let Jessica torture you."

"I heard that!" Jessica stood in the doorway. "I

wasn't going to torture him! I was just going to dress him up."

"Jessica is here. Run, Stinker!" I cried. Mitch and Steve and I all laughed.

"You'd better be nice to me," Jessica warned. "Or you won't get any presents from Santa." She stormed out of the room.

"I'm scared now!" I called after her.

"I got it! *Yes!*" Jessica squealed. She threw the Christmas wrapping to the floor. She held up another doll. I didn't know where she would put it on her shelf — she already has about twenty.

"Maybe with all those dolls, you'll quit torturing Stinker," I teased.

"I didn't torture him!" she shot back. "I just put your socks and one of your shirts on him."

Oh, brother, I thought. She dressed Stinker in my clothes — even after I told her not to.

But I didn't think about it for long. I reached for a big box with my name on it. I ripped away the wrapping.

"Awesome!" I cried. "New hockey skates!"

They were amazing. They were shiny black with blue stripes along the sides. Bright purple letters screamed MONSTER SKATES across the front of the box. BE A MONSTER ON THE ICE! it said under that.

"I can't wait to try these!" I exclaimed. I turned to my parents. "Would it be okay if I called some of my friends and got up a game?"

"Sure, Max," Dad said.

"Be home by four," Mom added. "Grandma and Grandpa are coming over for Christmas dinner."

"Deal!" Clutching the skates, I raced to the phone.

"I'm going too!" Jessica yelled. She dropped her new doll and began putting on her snow boots.

I stopped and whirled around. "No, you're not!" I shouted. "Mom, tell her she can't come!"

"Max is right," Mom told Jessica. "No one can keep an eye on you while Max is skating."

"No fair!" Jessica screamed. She ran to her room and slammed the door.

Mom sighed. "Just remember, home by four."

"Okay, Mom," I promised.

Eight of us met at the pond a half hour later.

"Cool skates," Steve said as we sat on a park bench changing out of our shoes.

I stepped onto the ice. What a glide these skates gave me! I took long, slow strokes. Then I picked up speed.

"Go, Max!" Steve called. He was playing on the other team. "You're really *moving*!"

I noticed my friends gaping at me as I zoomed by. These skates were making me go faster than

I ever had! I am a monster on the ice with these babies, I thought.

"Let's start," Mitch shouted.

I clutched my stick and slid into position with a *WHOOSH*. I was ready for action. "Just let me at that puck!" I declared.

Pete Stanton tossed the puck into play. I was on it in nothing flat. *SWISH, SWISH, SWISH* — my skates practically flew! I moved across the ice with that puck as if it were glued to my stick.

My muscles burned with power. No one could touch me. Steve tried to swipe away the puck, but with a quick flip, I swerved it out of reach.

Pete came up the other side. Hah! No good! I hustled the puck down the ice.

"Max! Yo!" Mitch yelled. He was open and wanted me to pass. But I didn't want to give up the puck. I knew I could take it all the way.

I did!

"Score!" I screamed. Mitch and Steve cheered.

"Awesome," Steve said. He skated up beside me. "Looking good out there, buddy."

"Thanks." But I didn't want to talk. I wanted to play! "Let's go!" I hollered. Steve and I skated toward the center of the pond.

Steve stared at me. "Relax. It's just a game."

"Yeah, yeah," I muttered. I picked up speed. With a spray of ice, I slid into position.

Mitch tossed the puck. Steve scooped it up and stormed down the ice.

"No!" I yelled. I took off after him. I pushed my muscles hard, harder! "Got to get that puck!" I cried.

I skated so fast, the other players were just a blur. All I could see was that puck.

And the kid who had it — my enemy!

Whoa! I came to a sudden stop. Ice chips spattered around the toes of my new skates.

Enemy? Steve? I shook my head. Steve was my best friend. And this was just a fun game.

It's not just a game, another voice inside me whispered. *Now get that puck!*

With a growl, I pushed off.

My heart began to pound. I wanted that puck. I wanted it bad. And Steve was keeping it from me.

I slammed into Steve. Hard. He went down.

I didn't care.

I dropped my stick and grabbed his coat as he fell to the ice. Then I did something that shocked me.

I grabbed Steve's coat and started shaking him! And while I did it, I growled again!

"Max! Max!" Mitch shouted from the other end of the pond. "Cut it out!" He skated toward us.

"Are you nuts?" Steve cried. He lay sprawled on the ice.

Part of me felt sick.

But part of me didn't. Part of me wanted to shake Steve harder.

"What are you trying to prove?" Steve demanded angrily.

A deep rumbling sound burst out of me. "Grrrah!" I snarled.

Steve and Mitch stared at me. I could see their eyes study me.

Hunching my shoulders, I skated toward the exit.

"Hey, Max, where are —" Mitch began to say as I passed him.

"Grrr!" I growled, and snapped my teeth at him!

Whoa! What was happening to me?

I was acting like a monster!

A monster on the ice . . .

The skates! I decided. My new Monster Skates were turning me into a monster.

I knew I had to get the skates off. I crossed the pond in record time. The kids scattered as I swooped by them. They looked terrified.

I didn't blame them — *I* was terrified!

My heart pounded as I stepped off the ice. I half-ran, half-stumbled to the bench where my shoes were.

I sat down and yanked off my gloves.

My hands! They were covered with thick, black fur!

I reached up and felt my face. It was covered in fur!

I yanked at the skate laces. I fumbled with the

knots. My furry hands were getting more and more clumsy. They were starting to look like paws.

Finally I pulled one skate off. "Hurry," I ordered myself. The next one came off. I heaved the Monster Skates away from me.

I stared at my feet. Huge, curved toenails had burst through my socks. Thick matted fur poked out the tops.

I felt my stomach lurch. Don't lose it, Max, I told myself. Somehow, I managed to sit still and take some deep breaths.

The skates are off. Will it work?

I shut my eyes and waited.

My skin started to tingle. The fur pulled back under my flesh. It didn't hurt — it just itched and tickled.

I stared down. The toenails were disappearing back into my feet!

I started feeling calmer. Less excited. Less angry.

"It worked," I said out loud. Yes! My voice was normal. No more growling.

I grabbed the skates and raced home. I was panting by the time I got to my room. I shoved the skates into the closet.

I needed to get back to the pond. I had to figure out a way to tell Steve what happened.

I darted out of the house and ran to the pond.

Luckily some of the kids were still there, including Steve.

When he saw me, Steve nudged Mitch. Soon all the kids were staring at me.

What was I going to tell them? That my new skates turned me into a monster?

"Steve," I said. "I'm really sorry, man."

He stared hard at me. "It's okay," he replied. "But why did you do that?"

"It was my — it was just a dumb joke," I said, hanging my head. I felt so stupid and scared. As I said, Steve is my best friend.

"Well, it wasn't funny," he snapped.

"I know. I'm really sorry," I mumbled.

"All right," he replied. "I guess we're going to skate more, okay? See you later."

Steve skated off with Mitch and Pete. I didn't have skates on, so I couldn't follow them.

I trudged home. Steve and I had fought plenty of times. But I had never tried to hurt him before. I wondered if I had lost my best friend forever.

I climbed the stairs to my bedroom. I put my hand on the doorknob.

And froze.

Sounds. On the other side of the door.

Oh, no! Jessica!

She was snooping around in my room again! Did she find the skates in my closet?

I flung open the door. She stood in the middle of the room.

"Jessica —" I cried breathlessly. "You didn't put on my skates — did you?"

"No way!" Jessica replied.

I breathed a sigh of relief.

"I put them on Stinker!" she cried.

"Huh?"

I turned as an enormous, growling creature leaped at me from the closet.

"Check him out!" Jessica laughed. "He's a Monster on the Ice!"

THE DOUBLE-DIP HORROR

"Wow, Wynona," Rachel whispered. "This place looks like an ice cream parlor!"

"Really!" I agreed. "From about a hundred years ago."

Rachel is my twin. The two of us have the same long dark hair. The same hazel eyes. The same mole on our right arm. We look exactly alike.

It was almost midnight. Rachel and I had arrived on a late flight. Now we were waiting in the empty lobby of Ice Cream Cone Ski Lodge for a desk clerk to wake up and check us in.

We came here because the coach of our school ski team put up posters. They said that Ice Cream Cone Ski Lodge needed junior instructors to teach little kids over winter break.

You'd teach six days. Then on Sunday, you could ski for free. You had to be thirteen to qualify. Rachel and I are thirteen. And you had to be a good skier. I don't mean to brag, but Rachel and I are super skiers!

The pictures on the poster made the lodge look so cool! All the slopes are named for desserts. There's Double-Dip Mountain, Banana Split, Whipped-Cream Peak, and Coconut Sprinkles!

"There's the clerk," Rachel said. "I'll go check us in. You stay with our stuff."

"Okay."

While I waited, I studied the pink-and-white-striped ceiling of the lobby. Posts painted to look like candy canes. Walls decorated with murals of giant ice cream desserts.

I could go for a chocolate shake right now, I thought.

I felt someone staring at me. I glanced up.

A boy stood on a balcony overlooking the lobby. He had on a yellow ski jacket. He looked about ten. His face was covered with freckles. He grinned down at me and waved. I waved back.

A few minutes later, Rachel hurried back over to me.

"He gave us keys to room 313," she said. Then we walked down a hallway to an old elevator. We got in, and it slowly rattled to the third floor.

Our room stood at the end of a peach-colored hallway. Room 313 had cotton-candy pink walls, bedspreads, carpet, and curtains.

Rachel and I called Mom collect to let her know we'd arrived safely.

"You're supposed to meet Margo, the head of the ski school, tomorrow morning at eight," Mom reminded us. "Don't be late!"

"I'm thirsty," I complained as we unpacked.

"Me too," Rachel said. "I have a warm soda in my backpack."

I spotted a plastic ice bucket on the pink chest of drawers. "There must be an ice machine," I said. "I'll go find it."

I took the ice bucket and walked back down the peachy hallway. I passed the elevator and turned a corner. I started down a long hall. The lights at the end of it had burned out.

It was dark down there. Really dark. My heart pounded as I walked down the hall.

A loud crash made me jump! I gave a startled cry.

Then I realized what the crash was — a bunch of ice cubes falling. I was closing in on the ice machine.

I came to an alcove. It was so dark, I barely made out the shape of a giant silvery ice machine.

I lifted up its wide metal door. I peered into the big freezer. Frigid air rushed out.

The ice cubes were way down at the bottom of the freezer. I grabbed the big metal scoop. I leaned over. I leaned so far that my feet came up off the floor. I jammed the scoop into the cubes.

Then something slammed into my back — hard!

I screamed as I dropped headfirst into the giant machine. My head hit the cold, wet bottom. I fought to turn myself right side up as my scream echoed inside the metal box.

And then I saw it. The door. It was coming down!

"No!" I cried.

I stuck out my hands. I pushed the door with all my might.

The machine spit out a shower of ice cubes.

They crashed onto my head.

Then, suddenly, the door gave way. I sat up. Grabbed the side.

Who pushed me?

I didn't see anyone.

I stumbled back to room 313. Rachel saw me and gasped.

My hair dripped ice water onto the cotton-candy pink carpeting.

"Did you just push me into the ice machine?" I demanded.

"Excuse me?" Rachel cried. "Why would I do that?"

"Well, someone did!" I snapped. I brushed past her on my way to the shower.

I let the hot water pound on my head for a long time. I tried to make sense of what had happened.

"I bet someone was playing a prank," I told

Rachel when I got out of the shower. "I bet they thought I was someone else."

We got into our beds. Then Rachel said, "Wynona? You want to do some real skiing on this trip?"

"Sure," I said. "But how can we? We only have Sunday off."

"It's a twin thing," Rachel said, smiling. "Let's take turns teaching at the ski school. There are lots of junior instructors. Only the desk clerk has seen both of us. We both have blue parkas and ski pants. Tomorrow morning, I'll go to the ski school alone. And you can hit the slopes. After lunch, we'll switch."

"Good plan," I said. "No — make that *great* plan!"

The next morning at eight, Rachel reported to Margo at the ski school hut at the foot of Coconut Sprinkles.

I headed for the ski lift up to Banana Split!

I met Rachel for lunch at a snack bar far from the ski school. We didn't want to be seen together.

"Banana Split is super!" I told Rachel. "You have to try it!" I smiled. "So, how did it go with Margo?"

"As far as she knows, there's only one of us," Rachel said. "I told her my sister had to stay home sick."

"Great!" I said. "So, tell me about the students in our class."

"Well, Annie tries really hard," Rachel began. "And Wes is getting the hang of turns. But Bobby Judd — what a brat! He kept pulling off my wool cap. He begged me for a private lesson. He's a pretty good skier too. I don't know why he's even in ski school.

"He's wearing a yellow ski jacket," she went on. "Watch out for Bobby Judd, Wynona. He's a terror."

Rachel filled me in on the other students as we ate. Then she wished me luck and took off for Banana Split.

I headed for the ski school. I reminded myself to say that I was Rachel.

Right away I spotted Bobby in his yellow parka. He was grinning at me.

A woman inside the ski hut waved to me from a window. She had to be Margo. She thought I was Rachel. Our plan was working!

I knelt down to help my group get into their skis.

Bobby skied by and whisked my gloves off my ski poles.

"Come and get me, Rachel!" he taunted me.

The other kids in the class didn't bother to look at him when he yelled. I guessed they were used to him acting up.

I took the class up a T-bar to the top of Coconut

Sprinkles. One side of it was a nice, easy slope. That's where I'd hold my class. The other side had a steep drop.

"Okay," I said. "Put your feet together. Bend your knees."

They did. All but Bobby. He skied away from the group. He darted around behind everyone else, waving my gloves in the air.

My bare hands were turning bright red from the cold.

"Plant your ski poles and pick up your left ski," I said.

"Try to make me, Rachel!" Bobby yelled from behind a pine tree.

I gritted my teeth. I tried not to lose it.

I was showing the kids how to turn when Bobby skied over. He threw my gloves in my face. "I want a private lesson!" he yelled.

"Fat chance," I muttered, pulling on my gloves.

I turned back to my class. "Okay, lean into your turns as you go down the hill. This slope is really icy and slick today. So dig in the edges of your skis. You first, Annie. Ready? Go!"

Annie started slowly down the slope. She veered to the left.

"Nice turn!" I called. "Now come back to center."

But Annie kept heading left.

Bobby started following Annie down the slope.

"Hey!" I shouted to him. "That's dangerous!"

Annie looked back at me. "What?" she called.

"Put your weight on your other ski!" I yelled to her.

Annie wobbled and took a slow-motion fall.

Bobby kept heading right for her. At the last second, he veered away. Then he raced for the far side of the hill.

"Wes!" I called. "Help Annie up! The rest of you, wait where you are! I'll be right back."

I pushed off with my ski poles and raced after Bobby. I sped around a tree. I skidded around a turn. I was going top speed.

Bobby was heading for the drop-off! He disappeared behind some trees.

I sped in his direction.

As I passed a big spruce tree, I saw Bobby stick out one of his skis — right in my path.

I swerved, trying to miss it.

I lost my balance. I circled my arms, trying to stay up. But it was too late.

I hurtled forward. I crashed onto the icy snow.

My skis flew off. I tried to plant my ski boot. But the crust of ice was too slippery.

I was sliding down the icy slope, headed for the drop-off!

The slope was a sheet of ice. I slid faster and faster.

The edge of the drop-off was close now. Really close!

Desperately, I lunged sideways, and slammed into a tree.

I lay still — inches away from the edge.

I tried to move my legs. But I was all tangled up.

Thoughts flashed wildly through my head. Bobby . . . ohhh! What I would do to that kid when I got up! If I ever got up . . .

Ten minutes later, I stomped back to the top of Coconut Sprinkles. I carried my skis over my shoulder. I'd have a bruise on my back where I'd hit the tree. But I was okay.

My class was there, waiting for me.

"Are you okay, Rachel?" Annie asked.

"I'm fine, Annie," I said. "Thanks."

Bobby popped out from behind a tree. He laughed loudly.

No one in the class laughed with him. They probably disliked him as much as I did.

Well, I thought. If they can ignore Bobby, I can too. And that's what I did for the rest of the afternoon.

That night Rachel and I ate dinner at different times. We were only together inside room 313. No one knew there were two of us.

When Rachel and I climbed into our beds, I said, "Hey, Rach? Tomorrow after ski school, let's give Bobby a private lesson."

"Are you crazy?" Rachel asked. "After what he did to us?"

"A private *twin* lesson." I smiled wickedly. "I'll take him up to Banana Split. You'll be hiding. I'll ski down the hill. Then you show up — from above! We'll keep taking off and showing up, over and over. He'll go crazy!"

"Good plan." Rachel smiled. "Let's do it!"

"Bobby?" I said the next day as my class lined up for the T-bar. "I'm free this afternoon. You still want a private lesson?"

"You bet I do, Rachel," Bobby said, grinning.

"Meet me on top of Banana Split at four," I told him.

But Bobby shook his head. "Make it Double-Dip."

"Double-Dip!" I exclaimed. "But that's a Black Diamond slope. Double-Dip is for expert skiers only."

"I know," Bobby said, still grinning.

"Okay, Bobby." I smiled back. "We'll make it Double-Dip."

When ski school ended, I hurried back to room 313. I told Rachel about the change of plans. She looked worried.

"But how will Bobby get down?" she asked. "He can't ski it."

"He'll have to take the lift *down*!" I laughed. "That will be so embarrassing!"

I took off for the Double-Dip lift.

Rachel was to follow in five minutes.

When I skied off the lift, I spotted Bobby right away. His yellow ski jacket was hard to miss. As always, he was grinning.

"Okay, let's go," I called to him. "Follow me."

I led the way across the mountaintop. I led Bobby into the Double-Dip woods. *Far* into the woods. I looped around a lot to give Rachel time to hide behind a tree above us.

"Wait here for a second, Bobby," I said loudly. "I want to make sure this trail is open." And I skied off down the hill.

As soon as I was out of sight, I stopped. I waited. I knew any second, I'd hear Bobby yell. He'd be totally freaked when Rachel skied down from above him!

I started quietly sidestepping up the hill. I had to be ready when my turn came to pop out and surprise Bobby.

The minutes passed. I didn't hear anything. I waited.

Nothing.

Finally I couldn't stand it any longer. I sidestepped to the spot where I'd left Bobby. But when I reached it, he wasn't there.

Neither was Rachel.

"Bobby?" I called. "Rachel?"

Nobody called back.

I called again. And again. But no one answered.

The sun was going down now. The light was

fading. I stood there, calling and calling. I started to panic.

Then I heard a faint cry: "Wynona!"

Rachel came skiing toward me.

"Where were you?" we both called at the same time.

"I've been here!" I said. "Right where I said I'd be."

"Here?" Rachel cried. "But this is the *far* peak! I've been waiting on the *near* one!"

We stared at each other. How could we have forgotten?

Double-Dip was named for its two identical peaks!

"Where's Bobby?" Rachel wanted to know.

"He was here when I left him," I told her.

"You think he skied down by himself?" Rachel asked.

I shook my head. "He couldn't. It's too difficult."

"Maybe he took the lift down," Rachel suggested.

"But," I whispered, "what if he didn't?"

We both glanced at the setting sun. We had to do something, and fast. Soon it would be dark.

"Let's ski down and see if we can find him," Rachel said.

"But what if he comes back here?" I asked. "Looking for us?"

Rachel sighed. "You ski down the mountain, Wynona," she said. "I'll stay here and see if he shows up."

"But . . ." I swallowed. "What if he doesn't?"

"I'll wait here for half an hour," Rachel declared, trying to sound calm. "Then I'll ski down. Go on, Wynona! Hurry!"

I pointed my skis down the mountain. I took off. Every second counted. The temperature was dropping. The trail was as slick as glass. I slid all over the place. But I kept going. We couldn't leave a kid up here to freeze — even an obnoxious kid!

At the bottom of the mountain, I skidded to a stop. I pulled off my skis and ran into the ski school hut.

"Margo!" I shouted. "Have you seen Bobby?"

"Bobby?" Margo frowned. "Bobby who?"

"Uh . . . I can't remember!" I groaned. "But he's lost! On top of Double-Dip! Call the ski patrol, Margo!"

Margo flipped quickly through her roll book. "No," she said, closing it. "We don't have a student named Bobby."

"Yes, we do!" I cried. "He has a yellow ski jacket. He's always grinning. His face is covered with freckles. Bobby . . . Judd! That's it! Judd."

Margo's eyes grew wide. She put a hand to her mouth.

"He hasn't been here for years!" she muttered.

"Who hasn't?" I yelled. "What are you talking about?"

Margo hurried over to her desk. She began rifling through a drawer. At last she pulled out an old black-and-white snapshot.

"Here," she said, handing it to me. "Is that Bobby?"

I squinted at the picture. "Yes!" I cried. "That's him!"

"I thought so," Margo said. "Well, we won't find him."

What did she mean? I stared at the picture. It was Bobby, all right. I flipped it over.

Penciled on the back was: BOBBY JUDD, 1954.

"Nineteen fifty-four?" I glanced at Margo. "I don't get it."

"Bobby Judd skied here every winter," Margo told me. "He came with his father and his twin brother, Ricky. The boys looked exactly alike. And they were twin daredevils. On their tenth birthday, they had a race on Double-Dip. They zoomed down the mountain. Bobby smashed into a tree. He was killed instantly."

"Bobby? Killed?" I said. "But . . . but he was here! I saw him!"

Margo shook her head. "You saw his ghost," she whispered.

"His *what*?" I cried.

"Bobby's ghost misses racing with Ricky,"

Margo told me. "At least that's what the old-timers around here say. So Bobby's ghost tries to lure a skier to the top of Double-Dip. Then he races that skier down."

Margo shook her head. "Some of the skiers don't make it."

"No!" I screamed. "But my sis — I mean, my . . . my friend is up on Double-Dip right now!"

"Don't worry," Margo said. "Your friend is safe."

"But the trail is solid ice! It's really dangerous!" I cried. "What if Bobby tries to race her?"

"He won't," Margo told me.

My heart pounded. "How do you know?" I demanded.

"Your friend is safe," Margo replied. "Bobby only goes after identical twins."

SANTA'S HELPERS

"Did you hear something?" I asked my sister Beth.

Beth peered up from the game of checkers we were playing on the living room floor. She listened. "No. I didn't hear anything," she declared.

"You did *too* hear me!" our little sister, Diana, shouted. "I said, can I play the winner?"

I didn't answer.

"Why won't you answer me?" Diana cried. "Why can't I play with you?"

I placed my hand on a red checker and made my move. "Because only humans can play checkers —" I started.

"And you're not human," Beth finished. "You come from Mars — not from Earth."

"Good one!" I gave Beth a high five.

My name is Spenser Mayhew — and here are the things I like to do. I like to play checkers with my sister Beth. I'm twelve and she's eleven, so we're a pretty good match. I like to play baseball in the schoolyard. And I like to go sledding in fresh snow.

But the thing I *really* like most is teasing my six-year-old sister, Diana.

I know. I know. It's not very nice. But it is a lot of fun. And it's so easy — because Beth and I look like Mom and Dad, and Diana doesn't look like any of us. And we don't let her forget it!

"Please let me play," Diana begged. "You two always play together. You never play with me."

I stood up and placed an arm around Diana. "Well, there's a good reason for that," I said softly. "Are you sure you really want to hear it?"

Diana's big brown eyes opened wide. She nodded her head yes.

"I don't know how to tell you this —" I paused. I took a deep breath. "But you're not really our sister."

Diana gasped.

"That's right." Beth gazed solemnly at Diana. "Mom and Dad found you under a rock! You weren't born — you were hatched!"

Beth and I broke out into a fit of laughter.

"That's not funny," Diana cried.

"Hey! It's twelve o'clock!" I said, ignoring her. "Mom told us we could go sledding at twelve! We'll finish this game later," I told Beth.

We bundled up in our new winter snowsuits. They were bright red, with green fur trim. Mom bought them for us on sale. *Really* cheap, she told us. That's because they're *really* ugly, we told her.

Mom met us at the door. She ran her hand over my green fur. "Nice," she said.

"Take me with you." Diana raced up to the front door.

"No!" Beth and I answered at the same time.

"Take your sister with you," Mom ordered.

"She's not our sister," I said, and Beth laughed.

"How many times have I told you not to tease Diana?" Mom frowned at me. "Take your sister," she said firmly. "She likes the snow. And she won't bother you — she's good."

"See — Mom said I *am* your sister. I knew I was your sister," Diana said as we made our way to the woods.

"Sorry, but you're not," I told her. "You can't be in our family. We all have red hair — and you have black hair. We have green eyes — and your eyes are brown. And we're all really short — and you're so tall. You're definitely not our sister."

"I am *so* your sister!" Diana yelled.

"No. No, you're not," I insisted. "We never lie. We always tell the truth."

"Wow! Look at all the kids up there!" Beth pointed up ahead — to the steep hill that led into the woods. It was the best hill in town for sledding.

"Hey, guys!" Our friend Ted waved to us as we reached the top. "Want to go down together?"

Ted jumped on his sled. We hopped on ours. We let Diana sit between us — and we took off!

The wind whipped through our hair as we flew down the hill. "This is GREAT!" Diana's cheers rang through the air.

I brought the sled to a slow stop at the bottom of the hill. Everyone jumped off, and I turned the sled around.

"Want to ride down again?" I asked Diana.

"Sure!" She nodded eagerly.

"Okay — but only if you pull us back up the hill."

"I can't pull the two of you!" Diana cried. "You're too heavy!"

"Sorry — but that's the deal," Beth said as we leaped back on the sled.

Diana stared down at us. She let out a sigh. Then she grabbed the rope and started tugging.

The sled didn't budge.

She tugged harder.

"This is fun!" Beth shouted as Diana tugged us up the hill.

When we reached the top, Diana dropped the rope. "My hands hurt." She rubbed her sore palms.

I grabbed the rope — and Beth and I took off!

"Race you to the bottom!" Ted yelled.

"Hey! Wait for me!" Diana cried out.

"Too late!" I shouted as we picked up speed.

We had a great run down the hill. We couldn't wait to race back down again!

"You're going to have a horrible Christmas!" Diana shouted at us when we returned to the hilltop. "Santa is going to know how bad you were. And he isn't going to bring you any presents!"

"Want to know the truth, Diana?" I stepped up to her. "There *is* no Santa Claus!"

"That's not true!" Diana balled her hands into two tight fists. "There *is* a Santa Claus! He brought me my ballerina doll last year!"

"Mom and Dad bought you that doll," Beth told her.

"You're lying!" Diana cried. "You're big, fat liars! There *is* a Santa Claus. There *is*!"

"No. It's the truth." I shook my head. "We always tell the truth. There is no Santa Claus."

"Well, *I* think there's a Santa Claus," Ted said. "Because you two sure look like elves!" Ted pointed to our bright red snowsuits.

Beth and I glared at him.

"Well, you do." He laughed. "You're too short to wear red snowsuits. They really make you look like elves. And those don't help, either." He pointed to our red-and-green boots.

"Mom bought them on sale," Beth grumbled. "We really hate them."

"You really hate what?" Mom trudged up the hill.

"Nothing, Mom," Beth replied. "What are you doing here?"

"It's getting chilly. I came to take Diana home," she answered. "But you two can stay. Just make sure you're home in time for dinner."

"Don't let them stay!" I heard Diana wail as they started home. "They wouldn't let me ride on the sled!"

"Uh-oh. Let's hurry. Before Mom changes her mind," I told Beth. We jumped on the sled.

Beth, Ted, and I raced down the hill all afternoon — until the sun began to set. As it dipped behind the trees, the day grew dark and cold. Ted and all the other kids headed home.

"Let's go down one more time." I checked my watch. "We still have a half hour before dinner."

"Wow! This is awesome!" Beth cried as our sled flew over the snow. Her voice sounded tiny on the big, empty hill. "We own the mountain!"

A few stars began to twinkle in the blue-gray sky. Except for the quiet *shush* of our runners gliding through the snow, the slope was silent.

We soared down, faster and faster.

The powdery snow was packed down hard, from the sleds that had raced down it all day. Our sled soared on the slick surface.

"We're going too fast! Slow down!" Beth cried. "We're coming to the woods!"

I tried to slow the speeding sled.

I threw my legs over the sides and let them drag through the snow. I pulled back on the rope hard, until it cut through my fingers.

Nothing worked.

We picked up speed on the slick, icy surface.

"I can't stop!" I yelled. "We're going too fast!"

"We're going to crash into the trees!" Beth screamed in my ear. "Turn! Turn!"

I tried to turn.

Too late.

The sled smacked into a tree, hard.

Beth and I tumbled into the snow.

"Great aim," Beth grumbled. "I told you to turn —"

"Hey! What's going on?" I cried — as a big net fell over us!

I peered through the holes — and gasped.

Four small men held the net over us.

Four small men dressed in red snowsuits and red-and-green boots.

It seemed impossible — but they looked exactly like elves!

"What are you doing?" I flailed my arms, struggling to escape. "Who are you? Let us go!"

The little men didn't answer. They shoved us into a big red bag — and started to drag us away.

"We can't see in here!" I cried out as Beth and I tossed inside the bag. "It's too dark!"

"Let us out of here!" Beth yelled, kicking at the sides of the bag.

The little men ignored us.

I punched the bag hard. "Where are you taking us?" I demanded.

The little men remained silent.

"Wh-where are we?" I asked one of the little men as I stepped out of the dark bag.

He didn't answer me.

I squinted, trying to adjust to the bright light. "What is this place?"

I gazed around the room. It was enormous — bigger than an airplane hangar. The high walls were lined from top to bottom with shelves. Shelves and shelves filled with dolls, trucks, trains. Every kind of toy you could imagine!

"Wow!" Beth stepped out of the bag after me. "A toy workshop!" she exclaimed.

Toy robots marched stiffly around us. Zigzagging this way and that, as the little men tested them out.

I jumped back — as a remote-control Jeep zoomed between my legs.

Hundreds of little men rushed about, painting dolls' faces, testing video games, sharpening blades on ice skates.

I stared at the little men in disbelief. They all wore red-and-green suits. Could it be? I wondered. Is this really a toy workshop? Are these little men really elves?

"This is too weird," Beth whispered. "Let's get out of here!"

I peered frantically around the room, searching for a way out. But I didn't see a single door or window.

"There is no way out!" I told Beth.

"We want to go!" Beth shouted at the elves. "Take us home!"

"Home! That's a good one!" An elf laughed. Then he grabbed my arm. Another elf gripped Beth's wrist.

"Let me go!" I yelled.

The two elves dragged us across the workshop. They pushed us through a narrow archway — into a small room lit by a blazing fire in a stone fireplace.

In the center of the room sat a wooden desk and a swivel chair with its back turned toward us.

"Here they are!" one of the elves announced.

The chair began to turn.

I gasped when I saw the red suit, the big belly, the white beard — Santa Claus!

"Here are the two elves who escaped!" the other elf declared.

Santa peered over his bifocals. "How could you leave here the day before Christmas? You know how busy we are!"

We stood in shocked silence.

"Put them on double work duty!" Santa ordered. "You two elves will work eighteen-hour shifts for the next five years."

"But — but this is impossible," Beth stammered. "You don't exist!"

Santa clutched his big belly and let out a deep laugh. "That's just what we tell people, to keep them from snooping around. It keeps the tourists away."

"But we're not elves!" I insisted. "We have a family back in Ohio."

Santa pushed his chair back and stood.

He crossed his arms behind his back as he walked up to us.

"Hmmmm." He circled us, studying us carefully from head to toe. "You look like elves."

He walked around us again. "You dress like elves."

He returned to his desk and sat down. "I've heard excuses before — but that is really lame. Now, get to work! You can have a two-day vacation five years from now — if you work hard."

Then he picked up a pencil, lowered his head, and began checking off names on a list.

An elf grabbed my wrist. Another one gripped Beth's arm. They tugged us toward the workshop.

"Wait!" I wailed.

I struggled free from the elf's grasp.

I ran up to Santa.

"I can prove we're not elves! I can prove it to you!"

"You can?" Santa glanced up from his desk. "Okay. I'll give you one chance. You have *one* chance to prove you're not elves."

"Is this the place?" an elf asked as Beth and I struggled out of the big bag.

"Yes!" I cheered when I saw we were standing on our front lawn. I turned to the elves. "This is where we live!"

"Yeah. Right." An elf smirked.

Diana sat on the front steps, shoveling snow, making a snow castle.

"Diana! Tell the elves who we are! Tell them you're our sister," I shouted.

Diana glanced up.

She stared at the four little men — and gasped. "Wow! Santa's elves!"

"Tell them you're our sister! Tell them!" Beth cried.

Diana slowly made her way down the steps.

She walked up to us. "But you always told me I'm *not* your sister! You said I'm definitely *not* from your family."

"Diana! This is no time for jokes! Tell them you're our sister!" I begged.

Diana turned to the elves. "They said I'm not in their family. And they told me Santa isn't real."

"You two elves are the worst liars I've ever met," an elf said.

"Big, fat liars." Diana nodded her head.

"Let's go." One of the elves shoved Beth into the bag.

"You've missed enough work."

"Tell them who we are! Diana, please!" I pleaded as an elf grabbed my arm.

"Bye! Merry Christmas!" Diana waved to me. "Tell Santa I've been good!"

ATTACK OF THE CHRISTMAS PRESENT

My uncle Billy is just about the coolest person on the planet. He's been everywhere, and he knows all kinds of weird stuff. So when I found out he was coming to our house for Christmas, I couldn't wait!

Uncle Billy is fun to be with, and he also gives great presents. He gave me a dinosaur egg once. And a scarab from Egypt. It's a wooden beetle with a hawk and a snake carved on the bottom. I inked mine and stamped my notebook covers.

No one else I know has a scarab, except for my older brother, Doug. Uncle Billy gave him one too.

Doug is fourteen, two years older than I am. We both have black hair, brown eyes, and gaps between our front teeth. He's a little taller.

The day before Christmas, Doug and I were playing checkers.

I hate playing checkers with Doug. I like to play fast and see what happens. Doug sits around and thinks about each and every move. He usually wins too.

Doug had been staring at the board forever, trying to figure out his next move. I was gazing out the window, waiting.

A taxi pulled up to the house.

Uncle Billy climbed out of the taxi. He was loaded down with suitcases and some bulging black tote bags.

Uncle Billy is tall and thin, with curly black hair, and he wears thick glasses.

I ran outside and hugged him. Then I helped him carry his bags in.

Doug just sat at the table, still thinking about his next move. He's a very serious game player!

We awoke at about seven on Christmas morning.

Everybody picked a place in the living room to sit. I plunked down between the tree and Uncle Billy. Then Mom took each present from under the tree and put it in front of the person it was for. We had to wait until she handed out all the presents before we opened any.

"Can't I open just one?" I asked. I always ask that.

"You know the rules, Jack. Just wait," Mom said. She always says that.

Finally she finished passing out presents.

I could tell just by looking at my pile that I

wasn't getting the skateboard I really wanted. Nothing was the right shape or size.

At least Uncle Billy's present would be interesting.

I ripped into the wrapping paper. Pretty soon the floor was covered with paper and ribbon.

Mom gave me three sweaters, some socks, and some underwear. BORING!

I also got a Walkman and a bunch of CDs. And some excellent basketball shoes, and a computer game called Trolls' Bane.

Finally I got to Uncle Billy's present.

I ripped off the silver paper and uncovered a really spooky wooden mask! It had long fangs, and three eyes, and a wild mane of red-and-white horsehair.

It was . . . *different*. I didn't own anything else like it. No one I knew did, either.

But I just didn't like it. It was creepy.

I set it down and watched Doug. He still had a lot of unopened presents. Doug opens presents the way he plays checkers — slowly.

He picked up each one and studied the box. Then he undid the tape. Then he pulled off the paper in one piece.

Then he studied the present before opening the next one.

Sometimes Doug drives me nuts.

He got underwear and socks and sweaters too. He got some books and a big set of colored pencils and a sketch pad. He also got good basketball shoes. He acted as if he liked everything!

His present from Uncle Billy was wrapped in dark blue paper. He saved it for last.

"Open it! Open it!" I yelled.

So he opened it verrry slowly, just to make me suffer.

Doug slipped his fingernail under the tape on the back and both ends of the paper.

Then he folded the paper up — as if he'd use it again!

He lifted the lid of the box and found another box inside. He studied it for a while.

I jumped up so I could see it too.

The box was bright purple and had Japanese writing with white outlines all over it. On the front, in English, it said: ROBOT TAG.

Through a clear plastic window in the box, I could see what it was. An action figure.

I had stopped playing with action figures. And Doug had *never* played with them. This one looked so cool, though, I wanted to get my hands on it.

It was a big silver robot with spikes around its neck, elbows, waist, and knees, and chains crossed over its chest. A spike like a rhino's horn stuck up from its helmet.

Doug opened the box and pulled the robot out.

It was jointed so you could pose it.

Doug flipped up the silver-gray faceplate to show the scowling face. The robot's mouth was opened wide, displaying lots of sharp, pointy teeth.

"That one is special," Uncle Billy said, watching us both. "At least, that's what the old guy at the toy shop told me."

"It's really cool, Uncle Billy," Doug said. "Thanks."

Doug was being polite. But I know him. I could tell he didn't like Robot Tag. For the first time ever, Uncle Billy brought us presents we didn't like.

We trooped into the kitchen. Mom made waffles. After breakfast, Uncle Billy said good-bye. He had to catch a plane to India.

Doug and I walked to the living room to pack up our presents and take them to our rooms.

I picked up the three-eyed mask. What could I do with it? I held it to my face and tried looking through the eyes. But the back wasn't carved out enough for a face to fit in it. I couldn't even wear the mask next Halloween.

I glanced at Doug. He was staring at the mask.

I looked at Robot Tag. What a radical robot!

"Trade you," Doug said.

"Really?" I shouted. "Really? Awwwright!" I slapped the mask in his hand, then grabbed Robot Tag.

Upstairs in my room, I checked out Robot Tag's joints. His ankles bent, his knees bent, his wrists bent, his fingers bent. He rotated at the waist, and his head turned. His arms could go straight out to the side, up, and forward. He could pose a hundred different ways.

I staged a fight with some old superheroes I dug out of the closet. Robot Tag beat them all.

I left him on top of the dresser when I went to bed.

I had just drifted off to sleep when I heard a scuffling, tapping noise. Maybe I'm dreaming, I thought.

Then I heard a thump.

I opened my eyes. And switched on the lamp.

Robot Tag was lying on the floor. I figured he must have fallen.

I left him there and turned the light out. I pulled the covers tight around me.

Then I heard more *TAP-TAP* noises. I reached one arm out and groped for the light. When I flicked it on, Robot Tag was still lying on his side.

A few inches closer to the bed!

I was getting a little freaked now. But I forced myself to calm down.

I have a wild imagination. And I knew it was running away with me. Toys don't come alive.

I turned the light off. And lay awake. Waiting.

Then I heard it again! *TAP, TAP, TAP.* Scuffle, scuffle, scuffle.

I clicked the light on fast!

Robot Tag was standing up! And he stood only a few feet from my bed!

I screamed. Then the action figure moved! It took a step toward my bed. Then another.

Maybe he has functions I don't know about, I thought. Maybe I tripped an on-off switch when I set him on the dresser.

I knew the sensible thing to do was to pick up the action figure and search for the switch. But I was too scared to move!

Robot Tag kept rumbling toward me. His spikes glinted in the light.

This was too creepy!

I took a deep breath. Then I flung off the covers and jumped out of bed. I ran from the room, slamming the door behind me. I darted across the landing and shoved into Doug's room without even knocking.

He was reading one of his Christmas books. He glared at me. "What do you want?"

"Robot Tag! He's alive! He came after me!" I shrieked.

"Don't be dumb," he replied.

"He was coming for me!" I insisted.

"You were dreaming."

I grabbed his pajama sleeve. "You have to see this!" I said. I didn't want to go back to my room alone!

He grumbled and shook his head. But finally he came with me.

Robot Tag stood motionless in the middle of the floor.

"Ooooooh, scary!" Doug said, rolling his eyes.

"He really was chasing me, Doug. Honest!" I insisted.

Doug sat down and picked up Robot Tag. He turned him over. I slid to the floor next to him.

Doug handed me the robot. I searched it for an on-off switch, but I couldn't find one.

"He was walking," I said in a small voice. Even *I* wasn't sure I believed it. Maybe I had been dreaming.

"If this is your way of telling me you want to trade back, forget it!" Doug said. "You're stuck with him!" He stood up. "Now go to sleep."

I put Robot Tag in the closet. I lay in bed a long time with my eyes open, staring at the ceiling and listening for more tapping noises.

I didn't hear anything. Finally I fell asleep.

When I woke up the next morning, I stretched in bed and sat up. And then I gasped.

Robot Tag stood on the dresser!

Had Doug sneaked into my room and put him there? No way. How would Doug know to look for him in the closet?

I walked over to the dresser and picked up Robot Tag. His eyes were squinting and mean-looking under the faceplate. The spikes around his joints were sharp. Too sharp for a toy, I thought.

I threw him back in the closet. Then I put on my new basketball shoes, ran downstairs, and ate breakfast. Afterwards, I biked over to my friend Rodney's house to find out what he got for Christmas.

By the time I got home, it was almost supper-time. I hurried to my room to clean up. I switched on the light — and stopped dead.

Robot Tag stood in the center of the floor again.

The robot raised one arm. His fingers opened and closed. Then the spikes around his neck, elbows, waist, and knees started spinning around — like tiny, biting saw blades!

Robot Tag took a step. *Tap.* Then another. *Tap.* Then he started moving toward me faster!

His faceplate flipped up. He gnashed his teeth at me!

No way was I dreaming this.

I started out the door. I turned to slam it behind me.

But the robot was too fast. It followed me out into the hallway.

GRRRRRRR!

His spikes were whirling!

His faceplate flipped up. He glared at me. He reached for me!

I ran back into my room and slammed the door. Then I yanked open my closet door and searched for something I could use to defend myself.

My hockey stick!

I grabbed it and whirled around. Just in time to see wood shavings flying from under the door.

GRRRRRRR! Robot Tag was using his whirling spikes to drill a hole in the bottom of the door.

A few seconds later, he came crawling through the hole. Baring his teeth.

TAP, TAP, TAP.

I waved the hockey stick at him, hoping I could beat him back.

But the robot grabbed the stick with both hands and squeezed. A hunk of stick broke off.

I jabbed him with it, and he broke off another piece!

My heart was pounding. I had to get away! I jumped as high as I could over Robot Tag and ran to the door. I yanked it open and ran downstairs.

Robot Tag came after me. I could hear his feet flying over the hall carpet toward the stairs. He moved so fast!

If I could just make it to the front door!

A sudden blur to my right. Robot Tag came sliding down the banister!

He thumped to the floor at the bottom of the stairs — and whirled around to face me.

He snatched at me with his hands. Then he lowered his head and aimed his rhino horn at me. He was about to charge!

I tripped on the edge of the living room rug and went down. Gasping for breath, I glanced back at the robot.

TAP, TAP, TAP!

I struggled to get up — but I was too late.

Robot Tag stood over my face! He raised both his arms. I closed my eyes.

And felt his hands slap me on the shoulder.

I opened my eyes.

The robot grinned.

"Tag!" he yelled. "You're it!"

ABOUT R.L. STINE

R.L. Stine is the most popular author in America. He is the creator of the *Goosebumps*, *Give Yourself Goosebumps*, *Fear Street*, and *Ghosts of Fear Street* series, among other popular books. He has written more than 100 scary novels for kids. Bob lives in New York City with his wife, Jane, teenage son, Matt, and dog, Nadine.